"Search," Chase to

The golden retriever sh the far end of the house. Keeping a hand on his weapon, Chase stayed close as the K-9 entered a room at the end of the hall. A nursery. Chase's stomach clenched.

Zoe Jenkins lay crumpled on the floor beneath a chunk of ceiling that had fallen. Chase could hear a baby crying.

His heart contracted in his chest. Was the woman dead? Swiftly he pushed aside the plaster. "Ma'am?"

She didn't move. The baby continued to cry, its pitiful wails muffled by the mother, whose dark brown hair shielded her face. Dash whined as if he, too, were worried.

With his heart in his throat, Chase knelt, hoping to find a pulse...

* * *

Mountain Country K-9 Unit

Terri Reed's romance and romantic suspense novels have appeared on the *Publishers Weekly* top twenty-five and NPD BookScan top one hundred lists and have been featured in *USA TODAY*, *Christian Fiction* magazine and *RT Book Reviews*. Her books have been finalists for the Romance Writers of America RITA® Award and the National Readers' Choice Award and finalists three times for the American Christian Fiction Writers Carol Award. Contact Terri at terrireed.com or PO Box 19555, Portland, OR 97224.

Books by Terri Reed

Love Inspired Suspense

Buried Mountain Secrets
Secret Mountain Hideout
Christmas Protection Detail
Secret Sabotage
Forced to Flee
Forced to Hide
Undercover Christmas Escape
Shielding the Innocent Target

Rocky Mountain K-9 Unit

Detection Detail

Pacific Northwest K-9 Unit

Explosive Trail

Mountain Country K-9 Unit

Search and Detect

Visit the Author Profile page
at LoveInspired.com for more titles.

Search and Detect

TERRI REED

Love Inspired SUSPENSE

INSPIRATIONAL ROMANCE

Special thanks and acknowledgment are given to Terri Reed for her contribution to the Mountain Country K-9 Unit miniseries.

LOVE INSPIRED® SUSPENSE
INSPIRATIONAL ROMANCE

Recycling programs for this product may not exist in your area.

ISBN-13: 978-1-335-48388-1

Search and Detect

Love Inspired
22 Adelaide St. West, 41st Floor
Toronto, Ontario M5H 4E3, Canada
www.LoveInspired.com

Printed in U.S.A.

And the Lord shall guide thee continually,
and satisfy thy soul in drought, and make fat thy bones:
and thou shalt be like a watered garden,
and like a spring of water, whose waters fail not.
—*Isaiah* 58:11

To the ladies of the Mountain Country K-9 Unit,
I appreciate all the brainstorming and support
as we brought the characters to life.
And a huge thank-you to the editorial team
at Love Inspired Suspense.
These continuities are a team effort.

ONE

Singing with gusto, Zoe Jenkins stood at her kitchen counter with a plethora of paleo-friendly ingredients spread out before her. The rhythmic banging of a plastic spoon against a plastic tray underscored Zoe's melody. Nine-month-old Kylie's chubby little legs and arms waved happily from her high chair, a vision in soft pink in the middle of the cheery yellow kitchen.

A sharp contrast to the weather outside.

The day was gray and chilly. Late fall in Wyoming could bring snowfall and freezing temperatures. So far, the weather had been holding at gloomy.

But life was good right now. Zoe's business was taking off, and she had Kylie. What more could she need?

The whisper of loneliness and quiet anxiety of raising a child alone stirred within her, but she wouldn't give them any ground, too afraid if she gave in, she'd end up weeping on the floor.

She wiped her brow with her forearm as she stifled a yawn. A glance at the clock confirmed it was nearly time to put Kylie down for her morning nap. Today Zoe would take advantage and rest, too.

Fatigue pulled at her. She was definitely burning the wick at both ends. In addition to being a single mom, she worked part-time at the Elk Valley Community Hospital as a registered dietitian helping patients with specific dietary needs. She also ran her own special dietary needs catering business out of her home. To top it off, she was spearheading the upcoming Elk Valley High School multi-generation reunion.

Raising her daughter alone meant juggling multiple responsibilities.

But it was better this way. There was freedom in being alone.

Again, a whisper of discontent knocked at her consciousness. She ignored the annoying sensation.

She'd learned not to rely on anyone except God. A familiar bubble of anger clogged her throat. She quickly took several calming breaths and forced the hurt and resentment back into its cage deep in her heart. Being dumped by her ex-husband five days after Kylie's birth had been a low blow.

Best to concentrate on the fact she had a growing clientele who kept her busy. She created delicious meals and delivered them to her clients' doorsteps, which allowed her to work mostly from home and be with Kylie.

As she handed Kylie a slice of banana, Zoe's gaze snagged on the stack of flyers for the upcoming reunion. There was still so much to do.

Her small committee had been working for months to put this event together. Despite the fact there were those in town who thought having a reunion with the Rocky

Mountain Killer still on the loose wasn't a good idea.

But the town needed to heal.

She'd been mourning her brother's death for ten long years. Seth had been one of the RMK's first victims.

It was time to honor those they'd lost and bring the town back together.

Or maybe she just needed this event to heal from her own heartache.

Kylie fussed, her cherub face scrunching up, a clear signal she was ready to be released from the high chair.

"Okay, sweetie pea," Zoe said. "I just need to fill one more box and then it'll be naptime."

She wrapped the prepared meal she'd made in cellophane and placed it inside a white catering box. She shut the lid, smiling at the sight of her business logo. A bright green *Z* above the words The Au Courant Chef—Zoe Jenkins. She set the box in the refrigerator next to several others. Later today she would bag the boxes up and drive them over to her client, Mayor Singh.

The trill of her landline startled her. She stared at the instrument sitting on the other end of the counter. Who would be calling her on that phone?

On the advice of her pediatrician, she'd had a landline installed after Kylie was born. Dr. Webb had said he always recommended one to new parents. Cell phones could run out of battery and be unavailable in the case of an emergency. However, a landline would always provide 911 with a physical address of where to send emergency personnel. She didn't have an answering machine set up and didn't intend to. She wanted the landline for calls out, not in.

Probably spam.

She ignored the ringing.

The phone went silent but started up again a few seconds later.

The insistent noise hammered at Zoe, grating on her nerves.

She quickly washed her hands. By the

time she turned the water off the phone had gone silent again. She breathed out a sigh of relief.

After packing the rest of the ingredients into the refrigerator, she moved to release Kylie from the high chair.

The ringing started up for a third time.

"Someone is sure persistent," Zoe said aloud. She stared at the phone. Unease slithered down her spine. Would they just keep calling until she answered? That would seriously mess with naptime.

With a growl of frustration, she grabbed the receiver. "Hello?" She couldn't keep the irritation from her voice.

There was a brief silence then a stream of distorted maniacal laughter, like from a creepy recording of a horror movie, filled her ear. Zoe held the phone away from her as the unnerving sound continued.

"Ugh!" Zoe slammed the receiver down. Prank call.

The world had turned upside down, and someone thought it would be funny to harass her on the landline. Someone needed to get a life.

Unsettled and beyond annoyed, Zoe picked Kylie up from the high chair and hugged her close. Singing a soothing tune, hoping to keep them both calm enough to nap, she carried Kylie to the nursery at the other end of the long hallway on the opposite side of the house.

The nursery was filled with fanciful motifs in bright cheery colors. Framed castles and unicorns and fields of flowers covered the walls. A white crib with bright pink and yellow bedding, a changing table painted in teal blue and a comfy rocking chair in cream with a floral print pillow sat beneath the window. A comfy and cozy space. The room brought Zoe joy. As did her daughter.

At the changing table, she continued to sing as she prepped Kylie for a nap.

A loud boom, low and deep, ricocheted through the house, rocking Zoe back on her heels. The entire house violently shook. Shock and fear exploded within her. She clutched a wailing Kylie to her chest and dove to the floor, covering her baby with her body.

Oh, God, spare us.

"Where are we on locating—" The sound of a distant explosion rattled the windows and raised the fine hairs on the back of FBI Special Agent Chase Rawlston.

He stood at the head of the conference room table in the Elk Valley Police Department for a task force meeting. The space had become the headquarters of the Mountain Country K-9 Unit. Sitting around the table were several of the men and women from various law enforcement agencies that made up the team tasked with locating and stopping a serial killer they'd dubbed the Rocky Mountain Killer.

The reign of terror had begun right here ten years ago in Chase's hometown of Elk Valley, Wyoming. Three young men, all recent grads of the high school, members of the Young Rancher's Club, had been murdered on Valentine's Day. Lured to a barn and shot dead. After that, the case had gone cold and a decade passed. But several months ago, murders in nearby states had the mark of the same killer. The victims were men originally from Elk Valley and connected in some way to the Young Rancher's Club.

The door to the conference room banged open and an Elk Valley police officer filled the open space. "There's been an explosion at a residence downtown."

Chase started moving while he said to the team, "Grab your gear and your K-9s. We need to find out what happened."

Everyone scrambled from their chairs to head to their assigned desks. Heart hammering with dread at the thought of the possible loss of life, Chase hustled out of the conference room ahead of the team.

"Could this be the RMK?" Deputy US Marshal Meadow Ames asked. Tall and fit from running, Meadow hailed from Glacierville, Montana, but was in Elk Valley to help with the RMK case. She, like several of the other team members, was staying at the Elk Valley Château until they closed the case.

"Not his MO." Detective Bennett Ford replied. Before joining the task force, Bennett had been with the Denver Police Department and still resided in Colorado but was also in town to help with the case. He was now married to the sister of one of their prime suspects. Chase had no doubt the strain on Naomi Carr-Ford was immense knowing that her brother, Evan Carr, was a wanted man.

But Evan wasn't their only suspect. The task force had discovered Ryan York had both means and motive. The man had a Glock 17 registered to him. A gun that could have fired the 9mm bullets used by the RMK. Matching slugs had been found at all the crime scenes, though investigators had never found the murder weapon. Chase had his sights set on Ryan as the culprit.

But both men had gone into hiding.

"He's changed his MO once already by stabbing a note into some victims' chests.

Why not use a bomb?" Elk Valley Officer Rocco Manelli pointed out as he hustled by. The local police officer who had followed in his father's footsteps had been a big asset to the task force. Rocco's father had been in on the original investigation into the Rocky Mountain Killer before dying of a heart attack with the case unsolved. Rocco had a personal interest in helping to bring RMK to justice.

Chase grabbed his flak vest and sidearm. His K-9 partner, a seven-year-old golden retriever named Dash, jumped up from the bed in the corner of the office clearly eager for some action.

"You ready to work?" Chase asked the dog. They had been partners since Dash was two years old. And Dash was trained in explosives detection, apprehension and protection.

Chase quickly leashed the K-9 and they headed out of the police department. The wail of sirens assaulted his ears. Smoke rose in the air, a dark plume that signaled destruction and stirred memories Chase had fought to lock away.

A deep grief slammed into him, nearly making him stumble as he and Dash ran several blocks toward the scene. He pushed thoughts of his late wife and child aside. He needed to stay focused and on his feet. Main Street in Elk Valley was slippery on this wet and cold late October day.

The temptation to pray, to ask God for there to be no casualties was strong, but Chase couldn't bring himself to do it. The chasm was too wide between him and God. And filled with hurt and sorrow.

With the team close on his heels, Chase skidded to a halt and drew in a sharp breath. The air was tinged with acid smoke. The left side of a small Cape Cod–style house located on a tree-lined street just off the main drag running the length of Elk Valley had been destroyed. Dash pulled at his lead and Chase followed. Dash led him toward the back northwest corner to what would have once been the kitchen and alerted. Some kind of incendiary device had been used.

Chase reeled Dash's leash in. He didn't want the dog to get burned by the flames licking at the sides of the house.

Concerned that there might have been occupants inside at the time of the explosion with no opportunity to escape, Chase redirected Dash toward the front door. Locked. Chase stepped back and then planted his foot with enough force against the door to bust the lock and send the door swinging open.

"Search," Chase said to Dash.

The golden retriever darted to the end of the lead, pulling Chase toward the far end of the house. Keeping a hand on his weapon, Chase stayed close to Dash as the dog moved straight to a room at the end of the hall that was quickly filling with insidious, dark wisps of smoke. A nursery. His stomach clenched. He fought back a sharp stab of grief.

A young woman lay crumpled on the

floor beneath a chunk of the ceiling that had fallen. He could hear a baby crying.

His heart contracted painfully in his chest. Was the mother dead? Swiftly, he pushed aside the piece of plaster. "Ma'am?"

The woman didn't move. The baby continued to cry, its pitiful wails muffled by the mother, whose dark brown hair fanned out, shielding her face.

With his heart beating in his throat, Chase knelt to touch the woman, hoping to find a heartbeat. Dash sat and whined as if he too were worried.

The moment Chase's fingers made contact with the woman's throat, she screamed and scuttled away from him, taking her child with her.

On his haunches, Chase raised his hands and stared into the dark, panicked eyes of a beautiful woman, clutching a baby girl to her chest. "Whoa, easy now. I'm with the FBI. I'm here to help."

The woman blinked, seeming to come out of her frantic state. She stared at Dash then back at Chase. "What happened?"

"Your kitchen exploded," Chase told her. He held out his hand. "Let's get you and the baby out of here."

The woman tilted her head as she stared at Chase. "I know you."

Chase had the sensation that he knew her, too, only he couldn't put a name to the face. But in a small town, everybody seemed to know everybody.

"You can trust me," he said.

She cocked an eyebrow. He thought for a moment she was going to resist, but then she held out her hand and allowed him to pull her to her feet. The baby pointed at Dash, babbling something that sounded like doggy.

Tamping down the swell of emotions rising through him, Chase tugged the woman and her child out of the room. Placing a protective arm around her shoulders, he guided her out of the house the way he'd come in. The smoke was thickening as more of the house caught fire.

The woman gasped at the sight of the destruction to her home. But he hustled her away before she could ask questions. He didn't have answers, and they needed to let the fire department get in and investigate.

Two paramedics rushed forward.

"They were in the house," Chase told them.

"We'll take care of them," the female paramedic said as she took hold of the woman and child, guiding them toward the ambulance bay.

Protective instincts surged. Chase wanted to accompany them, but he knew his place was not at their side. He turned his focus to the smoldering house.

"Do you know who that is?" Officer Ashley Hanson—now Officer McNeal—asked as she came to a halt next to him. Beside her stood her K-9 Ozzy, a black lab specializing in tracking.

Chase stared at the local cop who had been thrust onto his task force by her FBI honcho father. Chase hadn't been totally on board with the idea of a rookie being a part of the team, but she'd proven herself, and now Chase was thankful for her presence.

"I don't. But I should. Right?"

"Zoe Jenkins."

Chase's stomach dropped. The sister of Seth Jenkins. One of the three RMK victims from ten years ago. Along with his friends Aaron Anderson and Brad Kingsley.

It made sense that Zoe would recognize him considering he was the head of the task force created to uncover and capture the RMK. But he'd never met her; other members of the team had interviewed her as part of the investigation. She was familiar, though, whether because he'd seen her photo in the RMK file or that they'd both grown up in Elk Valley.

"Do you think the RMK is out to get her because of her brother?" Ian Carpenter asked. A former sheriff's deputy who'd spent time in the witness protection program, Ian had been recruited to join the task force, and he and Meadow were now engaged.

"We don't know that the RMK is in Elk Valley." Chase knew that the killer had traveled to Utah where one of his targets—the *main* target—lived now, but Trevor had eluded the RMK and was now in a safe house with his fiancée, a member of the task force. The RMK would not give up, though. That much Chase knew.

He saw the fire chief heading toward the house.

"Do a canvas of the area to see if anybody saw suspicious activity in the last day or so," Chase instructed the team.

He and Dash took off toward the fire chief.

"Heard you rescued a woman and child from the house," Fire Chief Fred Hawkins said.

"This wasn't an ordinary fire," Chase told the man. "Dash alerted. Northwest corner. I'm sure you'll find an incendiary device. I want it when you're done with your investigation."

"You got it."

"Good. I'll send my tech around to collect the evidence."

The fire chief nodded and went back

to work. Chase gazed at the house, then turned slowly, searching the area for any sign of someone too interested in the results of his handiwork. Residents all up and down the street had come out of their homes. Who had it out for Zoe Jenkins? Was this the work of the RMK? But that would mean the killer was back in town.

His gaze zeroed in on Zoe and her child settling into the back of the ambulance. A rush of concern hit him square in the chest. He and Dash hustled over. He climbed into the back and sat next to the paramedic without preamble.

"What are you doing?" Zoe asked.

"I need answers." Chase wasn't about to let Zoe Jenkins out of his sight. If the Rocky Mountain Killer was after the sister of one of his early victims, this might be the break they needed.

TWO

Sitting on the exam room table in the Elk Valley Hospital with Kylie in her arms, Zoe struggled to believe she and Kylie were alive. Her ears still rang with the phantom boom of the explosion that had destroyed most of her home. The feel of the ceiling falling on top of her as she shielded Kylie would haunt her nightmares.

Even though the paramedics had assured her that Kylie was unharmed, Zoe had insisted on seeing Kylie's pediatrician, Dr. Webb.

The fact that Chase Rawlston hadn't left her side except for a moment or two since he'd first found them in the nursery left Zoe feeling off-kilter.

Chase was a hometown hero and an FBI agent.

He'd been three years ahead of Zoe in high school, but she'd watched him play on the varsity football team alongside her now ex-husband, Garrett Watson.

Watching Chase pace across the room like a caged animal only ratcheted up Zoe's nerves. He was a big man with brown curly hair cut close, wide shoulders and long legs. He wore khaki pants and a dark jacket with the words FBI embossed on the back and the front pocket.

His dog, a beautiful golden retriever, was doing a much better job of being patient. The dog, too, wore an FBI vest, making him very official and adorable.

From the moment they'd entered the exam room, the dog had taken up a position by the door as if to make sure no one came or went without his knowing.

"Why are you here?" she finally asked when she couldn't take the silence any longer. "I'm sure you have more important stuff to be doing than waiting with me, right?"

Coming to a halt in front of her, he said, "I told you. I want answers."

Yes, he'd said as much when he'd unceremoniously jumped into the back of the ambulance. But then he'd stayed stoically silent. His dog had shown more interest in her and Kylie than the man who consumed too much space. His presence sucked up the oxygen in the bay of the ambulance and she'd found herself growing dizzy. Thankfully she was sitting now as she stared at him.

He had a commanding aura around him with his broad shoulders beneath his FBI jacket. His deep brown eyes held her gaze.

Did he blame her for the explosion?

An anxious flutter in her stomach had her wondering if she'd left a burner on. "I don't know what happened. I'm sure I turned the stove off when I was done cooking. But maybe I accidentally—"

Chase held up a hand, stopping her. "This was not your fault."

Zoe wanted to believe him. "But houses don't just blow up. I had to have done something to cause this."

Chase moved to sit beside her on the exam table, crowding her again, yet she didn't feel the need to move away. Odd.

He reached over to allow Kylie to grab a hold of his index finger. "May I call you Zoe?"

"Of course." She steeled herself for whatever he was about to say.

"Zoe, someone deliberately blew your house up."

She tucked in her chin, unsure she'd heard him correctly. "Say what?"

"My partner, Dash, is a trained bomb-sniffing dog."

Her gaze moved to the dog lying by the door. His big brown eyes watched her and Kylie.

She tried to wrap her mind around Chase's pronouncement. "You're saying your dog sniffed a bomb at my house."

"Exactly. Dash is very good at his job. He alerted the second we got close enough to the back northwest corner. Outside your kitchen."

The loss of her work, the meals prepped and ready to be delivered, stabbed through her and tears pricked the back of her eyes. "Why would someone do that?"

The dog rose to his feet and ambled over, putting his chin on Zoe's knee as if to comfort her. Kylie reached down her little chubby hands, grasping a handful of fur.

Afraid the dog would bite, Zoe quickly loosened Kylie's fingers. The dog just stared at them.

"He likes children," Chase said.

There was a wistful, sad note in his tone. Zoe searched his face, but he averted his gaze to his watch. "Where is this doctor?"

She remembered reading that Chase was the head of the task force searching for the Rocky Mountain Killer. There had been several articles in the local paper over the past eight months about the hunt for the murderer. A different sort of anxiety twisted in her chest "You're looking for my brother's killer. Do you really think you'll find him after all this time?"

"We're hopeful." Determination marched across his handsome face.

"Because he's active again," she said with a shudder of repulsion and fear.

"Yes. We're trying to figure out what triggered him to resurface," Chase said.

A shiver of fear slid down her arms. "You don't think it was the Rocky Mountain Killer who bombed my house, do you?"

"I can't rule out that possibility," he said.

Her breath hitched in stunned surprise. "But after all this time?"

"The mind of the killer is a mysterious and dark place," Chase said. "All we can do is try to stay ahead of him and attempt to anticipate his next move."

Distress squeezed her lungs, making her chest tight. "Did someone anticipate him coming after me?"

Chase gave a heavy sigh. "Unfortunately, no. You were not on our radar. But this opens the possibility that he'll go after the families of his victims."

Zoe tightened her hold on Kylie. She had to protect her child. "So, you're saying he's back in town."

"Not necessarily. The RMK's last known whereabouts was in Utah. I have a team still there searching for him. Until we know more about who might want to hurt you, I'm keeping an open mind and considering all prospects."

Zoe digested his words. If not the RMK, then someone else wanted her dead. "I can't think of anyone who would want to harm me and Kylie."

There was a soft knock at the door before it opened, and Dr. Webb, wearing blue scrubs, walked in. The older gentleman's concerned gaze took in Zoe and Kylie and Chase.

"Is it true someone tried to…?" He cut himself off with a shake of his head. "Zoe, the paramedics tell me they checked out Kylie and she's fine. But I'm glad you brought her in anyway. I'll do my own check."

Relieved, Zoe smiled. "Thank you, Dr. Webb. I dove on top of her. I just want to make sure she doesn't have any bumps or bruises that the paramedics missed."

Chase rose and moved toward the door. He made a clicking noise into his cheek and Dash scrambled to his paws. "We'll be right outside."

He and his dog left the exam room. For some reason, Zoe wanted to ask him to stay. Which was ridiculous. She didn't need him. Her days of relying on a man for her well-being were long over.

Chase stopped outside the exam room door. His gaze scanned the area, taking in the nurses' station and the various medical personnel going about their jobs. There were no discernable threats. He let out a breath, easing the constriction in his chest.

Being at a hospital with Zoe and her little girl made his heart ache, stirring the grief that was never far from the surface.

What was he doing here?

He should be checking in with the team, learning if there were any updates on the serial killer they were tracking.

They'd had the RMK in their grasp last month in Utah, but he'd slipped through their fingers. And they'd hit a dead end with their two prime suspects, who couldn't be located.

Evan Carr's alibi for the night of the original three murders had fallen apart when his then-girlfriend confessed in a recent interview that Evan had not been with her the whole night as she'd originally claimed. Which meant he'd had the opportunity to commit the crimes. Evan's sister had been humiliated by the victims—though one of them had simply been part of the group of friends—at a Young Rancher's Club dance.

Then there was Ryan York. His sister, Shelly, had dated Seth Jenkins, one of the Rocky Mountain Killer's original victims. From all accounts, Ryan was furious with Seth and his friends because of

Seth's treatment of Shelly. Shelly had committed suicide by taking sleeping pills not long after her breakup with Seth. A stronger motive than a supposed prank date that had gotten out of hand.

Chase firmly believed York was the killer. But he needed to prove it by capturing him.

Both suspects were tall and blond, which matched the description they had of the man who'd kidnapped the MCK9 task force's therapy dog Cowgirl, a labradoodle, who had been in training. They knew the RMK had the dog.

At least the killer had had the decency to leave Cowgirl's recent litter of puppies for the team to find and care for when they'd been searching for him in Utah. If only he would release Cowgirl. Chase worried about the labradoodle's well-being. But from the taunt-texts he'd received from the RMK, it appeared he was taking care of the dog.

The killer had taunted the task force on other occasions, too. He'd stabbed notes into the chests of two recent victims, Henry

Mulder in Montana, and Peter Windham in Colorado.

Notes that warned of more deaths to come. Sure enough, he'd killed Luke Randall in Idaho. And now he was gunning for Trevor Gage, Elk Valley's golden boy.

Trevor was now secured in a safe house with his fiancée, task force member Hannah Scott, a Utah highway patrol officer, and her K-9 partner, a Newfoundland named Captain. Chase was sure the RMK didn't know where Trevor was located. He'd called the team back to Elk Valley after securing his protection last month.

He needed to focus on the RMK investigation.

Yet, he hesitated to leave the hospital.

Call it a gut instinct or hard-earned experience, but something compelled him to stay.

Could the RMK case and the bombing of Zoe's home be connected?

A question that kept running through his mind.

Until he had the answer, he had to provide protection to the innocent victim and her child.

He took out his phone and pressed the speed-dial number for his boss in Washington, DC.

On the second ring, Cara Haines answered. "Rawlston. Good news, I hope."

Chase winced. He'd worked for Cara back when he lived in DC. She was the reason he was heading the task force. And she knew him well enough to know he wouldn't call unless it was important. "No. But there's been a development."

"You have the whereabouts of the RMK?"

He shook his head with a grimace. "Still unknown. But the sister of one of the RMK's first victims was attacked today. Her house was rigged with an explosive. I can't say for certain there's a connection but—"

"But you want to pursue the investigation," Cara stated.

"I do, and I'll need the task force's help," he told her.

There was a moment of silence as she considered.

"All right. But I don't want the RMK case to lag," she said firmly.

"No, ma'am. It won't," he assured her.

"Good. Keep me informed," she said. "And Rawlston, I've alerted Deputy US Marshal Sully Briggs that we will utilize the marshal service when you capture the RMK."

Chase appreciated her confidence in the task force's success. "I'll keep Deputy Briggs updated."

"Anything else?" Cara asked.

"No, ma'am, that's it."

"In case I haven't said it lately, Chase, you're doing a good job. Elsie would be proud of you," Cara added, her voice softening.

Chase squeezed his eyes shut against the pain her words caused. Squaring his shoulders, he said. "Thank you."

"Okay, then," Cara said. "Back at it." Cara hung up.

Chase pocketed his phone just as the

door behind him opened. He steeled himself against the onslaught of emotions battering him. He had to stay detached, in control and vigilant. Anything less could result in tragedy. An outcome he would avoid at all costs.

As the doctor examined Kylie, Zoe ran through possible culprits or reasons why somebody would go to such destructive lengths to hurt her and Kylie. She tried really hard to be a good person. She may not be the warmest of people, but she certainly had no complaints from her clients or her patients here at the hospital. The only person who was disgruntled with her was her ex-husband. But Garrett wouldn't resort to attempting to kill her and his child to get out of paying child support and alimony. Would he?

"You can get her dressed," Dr. Webb said with a gentle smile. "She's perfectly healthy and normal. Not even a scratch or any sign of trauma." Dr. Webb patted Zoe's shoulder. "Good job protecting your daughter. What about you? The paramedics said you might have some abrasions on your back from falling debris?"

Zoe barely felt an ache where the portion of the ceiling had fallen on top of her. She would probably have a bruise. But the paramedics assured her nothing was broken. "I'm fine. Now that I know Kylie's all right, we'll get out of your hair. I know you're busy."

"I am always here for my patients," Dr. Webb said.

He opened the door to the exam room revealing Chase and his dog standing guard. Zoe smiled at the sight of the two males. Did he really think somebody would break into the exam room and try to harm her?

The thought sent a shiver traipsing down her spine. She didn't like this feeling of vulnerability stealing over her. Would the person come after her and Kylie again?

With hands that shook, she quickly dressed Kylie and joined Chase and his dog in the hallway.

A nurse in scrubs rushed up.

Chase held up a hand to stop her from reaching Zoe. A protective move that made Zoe's heart bump.

"Zoe," Haley Newton said. Her strawberry-blonde hair was pulled back into a tight bun at the nape of her neck. Her bright blue eyes were wide with concern. "I just heard what happened. It's good to see you uninjured."

"Thanks," Zoe replied.

Haley gave Chase a thorough once-over. "You're Chase Rawlston. I remember you from high school."

Chase arched an eyebrow. "Good memory. And you are?"

There was a flash of disappointment in Haley's eyes that she masked with a smile. "Haley Newton. I was a grade behind you. Are you back in town for the reunion?"

Zoe refrained from scoffing. Apparently, Haley hadn't read the *Elk Valley Daily Gazette*, which kept a running article on the Rocky Mountain Killer investigation. More than once Chase's name had been in the paper along with his team, several of whom were local to the area.

"Not exactly," Chase told her.

Haley turned her focus back to Zoe. "Are you and Kylie okay? Have you let Garrett know?"

Zoe gritted her teeth against the mention of her ex-husband but managed to say, "Not yet. And we're fine."

Haley reached out to run a finger down Kylie's cheek. "One would think this little bundle of joy's father would want to know if she was okay."

"One would think," Zoe repeated. But she couldn't say Garrett would care considering he'd walked out of their lives without so much as a backward glance. "I appreciate the concern, Haley. But we really have to head out now."

Haley stepped back. "Of course. Let me know if there's anything I can do to help you."

"I will," Zoe said, grateful for her colleague's concern.

Haley gave Chase another curious glance

before nodding and hurrying down the hallway.

Chase put his hand Zoe's shoulder. She reflexively stiffened at the contact.

He immediately lifted his hand. "Sorry."

"No, I'm sorry," Zoe said. "I'm just a little rattled from the explosion."

Chase gave her a measured look. "Garrett? As in Garrett Watson? He's your ex?"

Zoe winced. "Yes."

There was a speculative gleam in Chase's eyes. "Let's get out of here so we can talk."

They started walking toward the exit. Then Zoe came to a halt. "I have nowhere to go."

"Your parents?"

"They moved to Florida not long after Seth's murder," she said. "I have responsibilities here. I can't just head south."

Chase pushed open the exit door. "We'll think of something. But we can't do it on an empty stomach."

"I'll have to stop at the bank and see if I can withdraw some money," she said. "My purse with my ID and credit cards had been on the dining room table. They're now probably blown to bits. Along with the mayor's meal order. I'll have to contact him, too. I'll need to get a new cell phone. And clothes. Everything."

"We'll get you all situated in time," Chase told her. "But for now, let me treat you and Kylie to lunch."

A heaviness settled on Zoe's shoulders. It wouldn't hurt to accept his offer. She would pay him back as soon as she could. "The Rusty Spoke has sweet potato fries, which are Kylie's favorite."

"Then that's where we'll go."

The Rusty Spoke had a busy lunch crowd. The dim interior and booths lining the walls were perfect for some privacy. The low hum of conversation from the other patrons didn't drown out the soft country tunes playing from hidden speakers. Zoe waved to one of the waitresses, Jessie Baldwin. Their grandmothers had been friends before Zoe's grandma passed away.

Jessie was in her early twenties and wore

jeans with a Western-style shirt. Her dark hair bobbed about her chin as she moved. "Hi, Zoe. Sit where you'd like." Jessie eyed Dash. "Cool, a working dog. Can I get him some water?"

"Please." Chase pointed to an empty booth. "Let's take that."

Zoe nodded and let him and Dash lead the way. They wound around the tables in the middle of the floor toward the last empty booth. She felt conspicuous, like everybody in the place was watching her. Did everyone in town know that somebody had just blown up her home?

She glanced around, tightening her hold on Kylie. Was one of these people the bomber? She recognized most of the local patrons. But why would anyone want to hurt her?

Blowing out a breath, she silently admonished herself. She was being paranoid and ridiculous. Chase had just told her that the RMK was last seen far away in Utah. He wouldn't come back to Elk Valley.

Yet unease prickled the skin on the nape of her neck.

Zoe slid into the booth and settled Kylie on her lap. Kylie's chubby little hands banged against the wooden tabletop. Dash sat beside the booth.

Jessie approached the table and set a bowl of water in front of the dog, he immediately lapped it up.

"Zoe, we heard what happened," Jessie said. "Are you okay? I know my grandma has already started a prayer chain."

Heart thumping with gratitude, Zoe smiled. "We're good. Thank you for asking. And tell your grandma thank you, as well. We could use all the prayers we can get."

Jessie gave her a sympathetic smile, took their drink and food orders and hustled away.

"I don't know what we're going to do," she said aloud. "If what you suspect is true, that someone deliberately tried to blow me and Kylie up, it's not safe for us to stay with anyone we know. And I can't afford a room at the Elk Valley Château for an extended period of time."

"No responsibility is worth your life. You could go to Florida."

Zoe heaved a sigh. "I guess that's what we'll have to do." She frowned as concern darkened her thoughts. "But what if the person who wants to harm me follows me there? Then I'm just putting my parents in danger, too."

Chase rubbed his chin, drawing her gaze. He had a nice jawline with a hint of a beard. His brown eyes were warm like caramel sauce.

Somewhere in the back of her mind, she recalled someone saying he was a widower. She wanted to ask but thought that would be rude.

Besides, she shouldn't be curious about Chase. She didn't want to become attached to him in any way. But at the moment, she was having to rely on him, and that fact grated on her nerves. "I know God will provide. I need to be patient. This is all just so new and surreal."

Chase's hand dropped to the table. "Yes, patience would be good here. We'll need to come up with a plan. As for God providing—it's a nice sentiment but in my experience that doesn't really happen."

"In your experience?" She hated to think of him so jaded. Was he referring to his wife's death? Or to his job? "I would imagine as an FBI agent you've seen some horrible things."

He shrugged. "I have."

"This world can knock us down," she said. "But God is always reaching out to lift us back up."

A slight scoff lifted one corner of his mouth. "If you say so."

"I've experienced it," she told him. "When I was at my bleakest, I felt God's presence. He surrounded me with good people. And opened doors I hadn't even known were there."

Chase tilted his head. "Are you referring to Garrett and your divorce?"

Her stomach knotted. "I am."

"Tell me what happened," Chase said, his voice hard.

Zoe tucked in her chin. "I don't think rehashing my failed marriage will be productive."

"I'll be the judge of that," he said. "This incident today could very well be related to your ex-husband."

His words were a punch to the gut.

THREE

"Unlikely," Zoe said aloud, answering her own question. The clang of utensils against dishes mixed with the murmur of conversations around the restaurant. Zoe angled her back toward the other diners while keeping a firm hold on Kylie, who squirmed to be set free from Zoe's lap. "Garrett is many things… I can give you a litany of faults. But I don't believe he would do this. He wouldn't have the know-how. Nor would he expend that much energy on learning to make a bomb."

"You'd be surprised what people can do given the right motivation," Chase replied, clearly unconvinced by her argument. "How did you and Garrett meet?"

She sighed. Chase wasn't going to drop

the subject. "When I returned after college to take a job at the hospital, I bumped into Garrett one day at the hardware store. We got to talking and he asked me out. Of course, I knew who he was. He was in your class and on the football team. He had gone to work for his father and was in the process of taking over the business so his dad could retire. He was charming and good-looking." She shook her head. "I wanted to put down roots."

"How long were you married?"

"Just shy of seven years," she told him.

"What happened to break you up?"

Gritting her teeth against the spurt of anger tightening her throat, it was a moment before she could speak. She bounced Kylie on her knee and allowed the love for her baby to push back the resentment wanting to take hold.

"I became pregnant," she said. "I knew Garrett wasn't interested in starting a family while he was building up the business he'd taken over from his dad. He'd wanted to expand. In the beginning, I was fine with waiting. I had my own career to think of but then I ended up pregnant. I never imagined he'd abandon me."

She scoffed, remembering Garrett's reaction when she'd told him the news. "He was livid. Accused me of cheating." Hurt spread through her chest at the accusation.

Chase's expression didn't change, which helped her to continue.

"Garrett confessed that in high school he had an injury and the doctors told him he would most likely not be able to father children. He kept that from me. I might not have married him had I known. I can assure you, Kylie is his child. He even insisted on a paternity test, which only confirmed what I already knew."

Chase shook his head, his disdain clear. "He still didn't want to be a father?"

"No. He thought children would—oh, I don't know. Cramp his style. He liked being able to party whenever he wanted. To go on trips at the last moment. Usually without me. My job at the hospital wasn't as flexible then."

"He didn't deserve you or Kylie," Chase said in a tone full of certainty.

His words were a soothing balm that she quickly pushed away. She couldn't get sucked into Chase's charm. She'd fallen for a handsome man's charm once before and it had ended in disaster. Though she knew, logically, it wasn't fair to compare Chase to Garrett. They were as opposite as night and day. Weren't they?

She really didn't know Chase. Of course, she'd known of him for years, just like she'd known about Garrett before they'd started dating. Ha! Look how that had turned out. Chase could be saying what she wanted to hear in an effort to pry information from her. He had a job to do, after all.

What did it say about her that she was suspicious of his kindness?

"I want you to think back over the last few days," Chase said. "Was there anything suspicious that stood out to you? People in your neighborhood whom you've never seen before? A car that drove by more than once that didn't belong there?"

"I can't think of anything out of the ordinary." She paused. "Wait, that's not true. A few minutes before the house exploded my landline rang. A prank call."

His eyebrows rose. "What did the caller say?"

"Nothing." Irritation laced her words. "It was just this weird laughter that totally wigged me out."

"Laughter?" He considered for a moment then asked, "Male or female?"

Zoe shook her head with a shrug. "I couldn't tell. I hung up." Apprehension squeezed her chest. "I took Kylie to the nursery. A few minutes later…"

She shuddered at the memory. They'd come close to dying today. If it wasn't for Chase… "Thank you, by the way. I don't think I said that earlier. If you hadn't found us, I don't know what would have happened."

Chase reached across the table and gently took her hand. "You're safe now."

Warmth engulfed her. She stared at their joined hands. His was so much bigger and tanned, compared to her smaller hand that very rarely saw the sunshine. Her heart gave a little jolt. She resisted the urge to curl her fingers around his calloused ones, to cling to him. Instead, she extracted her hand and brushed back Kylie's hair.

Jessie returned to the table with their food and beverages. Zoe was thankful for the distraction as she fed Kylie sweet potato fries and picked at her own garden salad.

Chase had no problem devouring his cheeseburger and fries. Then he said, "Let me hold her while you finish your salad."

Surprised and grateful, she handed Kylie over the table into his capable hands. He bounced Kylie on his knee while Zoe ate. The nine-month-old was content, her eyes wide taking in the room, clearly undisturbed by being held in the arms of a stranger.

Zoe found herself distracted watching this big man with her child. He did well with Kylie, holding her firmly but also giving her wiggle room. The way a parent would.

Giving herself a shake, Zoe finished eating and took Kylie back so that Chase could slide from the booth and pay the bill.

He held out his hand to Zoe. "Come on. I know a place where you'll be safe."

Appreciating his gentlemanly manner, she grasped his hand and attempted to awkwardly slide out of the booth with Kylie in her arms. Chase quickly plucked Kylie from her and settled her on his hip. He looked so natural holding her, like he'd been born to be a caregiver. A father.

For a moment, all Zoe could do was stare.

Kylie touched Chase's face and he kissed her little fingers as they skimmed over his lips. His chuckle resonated through Zoe as she slid out of the booth and reached to take Kylie back. "She likes you."

He made an affirmative noise in his throat and headed toward the exit. Zoe watched his back wondering about his life.

Was he seeing someone? Or was he still grieving his wife?

Ack! She had no business contemplating such questions.

At the door, Jessie hustled over with a to-go bag that she thrust into Zoe's free hand. "A snack for Kylie."

Touched by the younger woman's kindness, Zoe said, "You didn't have to—"

Jessie waved away her protest. "I know. We all want to be there for you, Zoe. We look after our own." She lightly touched a fingertip to the end of Kylie's nose. "I'm looking forward to the reunion. I bought a new dress."

Glad to know Jessie was eager to attend, Zoe gave the younger woman a quick, one-arm hug. "Thank you."

Emotions surged and Zoe blinked back tears as she pushed through the door into the late October afternoon. The air was crisp and filled her lungs.

"You okay?"

Chase's softly asked question drew her gaze. The warmth in the depths of his eyes had her saying, "It's almost my brother's birthday, which is why I advocated for the reunion to be in October. Losing Seth to the RMK ripped my family apart. I was his sister. I should have protected him."

Chase shook his head. "Don't take on that type of guilt. The only one responsible is the killer."

She appreciated his words, appreciated his patience with her. "My parents couldn't stay here in Elk Valley. It was too painful, you know. Memories everywhere. But I returned after college. I didn't want to forget my brother."

"I'm sorry for your loss," Chase said. "The tribute reunion will honor Seth and the other victims. The committee hopes the community will be brought together and those who've lost a loved one will find some comfort.

"A commendable reason for the reunion," Chase stated.

His praise was unsettling. "Where to?"

After a barely discernible hesitation, Chase said, "A safe place."

Hugging Kylie close, Zoe had no choice but to follow and trust him.

How long would it take him to find the bomber?

After a stop at the Elk Valley police station to check in with the team, Chase drove Zoe and Kylie to his family home. He led them up the front walkway, noticing the grass needed to be mowed. The shrubs rimming the porch could stand a trimming. The rosebushes were bare but still thorny under the front window. They reached the varnished wood front door of the house he shared with his father. There was no safer place in Elk Valley that he could think of, beyond the police department, than here.

He wouldn't think about how hard it would be to have a mother and child underfoot, stirring up memories that he worked hard to suppress.

What would Zoe think of the place? Why did he care? "It's not lavish, but you'll be safe here."

"Whose house is this?" she asked, hitching Kylie higher on her hip.

"My dad's," he admitted with a bit of trepidation. "And mine, when I'm in Elk Valley."

She blinked up at him, her pretty eyes searching his face. "This is unexpected. Is this your childhood home?"

"It is."

Her mouth dropped open slightly. "Are you sure we won't be in the way?"

"Not at all." He infused assurance into his tone even though a bout of nerves ripped through him. "My father will be happy for the company."

His father had been ecstatic, actually, when Chase had called him from the police department to let him know he would be bringing Zoe and Kylie home. He'd been quick to impress on his father the scope of the situation. He didn't want Liam Rawlston to get the wrong idea and believe that Chase had a personal interest in Zoe and her baby girl.

Nothing could be further from the truth.

Yes, it was his job to keep Zoe and her baby safe, and he would. But his heart had been ripped out with the death of his wife, Elsie, and son, Tommy. Now there was a gaping hole he had no intention of filling. Forming an emotional attachment wasn't something he could allow. He couldn't ever go through that kind of pain again.

Zoe preceded him into the house with Kylie on her hip.

The sensation of being watched itched over Chase's flesh like hairy spider legs. He didn't like it. He paused and glanced back over his shoulder, taking in the modest homes lining both sides of the road. Several cars were parked at the curb or in driveways, but he couldn't discern any occupants. No window curtains fluttered with curious neighbors. Nothing seemed out of place on their quiet residential street. The police station wasn't far, an easy walk.

He glanced down at Dash who stared up at him waiting for the release signal for him to go inside the house. The dog wasn't alerting or showing any sign of distress that would indicate a threat close by. Chase trusted Dash implicitly. He may be a bomb-sniffing dog, but he was also well-versed in protection and apprehension. He'd made sure of that when Dash was younger.

"Release," Chase murmured, and they went inside.

Chase shut the door behind them and let his senses adjust. Everything was familiar and comforting. The same artwork on the walls, the same furniture, and the same beige carpeting from his boyhood. The only big difference was the large screen smart television in the corner. His gaze zeroed in on Zoe, who had moved to the worn brown leather couch and sat with Kylie on her knee. His father was nowhere to be seen.

"Dad," Chase called out.

His father emerged from the kitchen, wearing an apron over his customary chino pants and plaid button down, and wiping his hands on a towel. "I didn't hear you come in."

Liam undid the apron and set it and the towel over the back of a dining room chair. His father walked with a slight limp, left over from his days with the Elk Valley Fire Department. Burn scars had ravished his flesh on both legs and his right hip. The last fire he'd worked had almost killed him.

"You must be Zoe," Liam Rawlston said, holding out his hand.

"I am." Zoe took his hand in her delicate one for a quick shake.

Liam moved to sit in his favorite chair. A striped recliner that was a throwback to the seventies. "Chase tells me you've had a bit of trouble. And you need a safe place to stay. I can promise you, we will protect you."

Zoe bounced Kylie on her knee. "I appreciate this. Really. It just feels like we're an imposition."

Chase came fully into the living room from the entryway. "Not at all. My father's former FD but he's also a decorated Marine."

"Go on now, Chase," Liam said with a grin. "You're going to make me blush."

Zoe laughed, a soft sound that curled around Chase's heart.

Abruptly, he turned and headed for the kitchen, saying over his shoulder, "Come on, Dash. Time to eat."

Contrary to what he'd told Zoe, this would be difficult for him. As he'd sat across from her and her little girl, he'd been charmed. Zoe was so attentive, and Kylie was adorable. His heart ached with tenderness when he'd held her. So tiny and perfect. So vulnerable. Having them in his home would be an adjustment. One he'd never expected to make. The need to see to their protection personally wouldn't be denied. They were in grave danger, and he couldn't think of a safer place in town to house them.

The house line rang, and he heard his father answer and then tell Zoe the call was for her. After dishing out Dash's food, Chase returned to the living room. Liam held Kylie while Zoe talked to someone on the phone. Who could possibly know she was here?

Wariness crimped the muscles in Chase's shoulders. "Who is she talking to?"

Was it the mysterious bomber? Had the person who called her right before the bomb went off discovered she was staying with Chase and his dad?

"It's Pastor Jerome from the Elk Valley Community Church," Liam told him.

Unexpected and unwanted. Chase had no use for God or faith. Not after the tragedy that had taken his wife and child from him. Even as the thought stampeded through his mind, guilt stomped in, reminding him the blame for Elsie and Tommy's death lay squarely on his shoulders.

"How does the pastor know she's here?" Chase asked his father.

Liam shrugged. "When I got the call for donations from Martha Baldwin, I mentioned you were bringing Zoe here. Was that not okay?"

Chase cringed. He supposed in a small town like Elk Valley word would spread quickly about Zoe and Kylie staying with the Rawlstons. He'd have to consider moving her out of town. Though he doubted she'd go. Hadn't he just told her she'd be safe here?

And she would. He'd make certain.

Focusing on Zoe, Chase could see whatever was being said on the other end of the line was making Zoe happy. She thanked Pastor Jerome and hung up.

"The church has gathered donations for Kylie and me," she said. "We need to head over there and pick up what they have so far. Neither Kylie nor I have clothes."

Liam hefted Kylie up on his shoulder. The little girl snuggled in close, sucking her thumb.

Meeting his father's gaze and seeing the understanding in Liam's eyes made Chase's heart pound. His father knew how hard having Kylie around was going to be for Chase. For them both. Chase had lost a son and Liam a grandson. The baby was a reminder of their sorrow.

Yet, Kylie was such a sweet little one.

Her wispy brown hair sported a tiny pink bow that matched her pretty pink outfit smudged with dirt from the explosion.

Kylie held no resemblance to the tow-headed bruiser of a boy Tommy had been. Nor did Zoe resemble Elsie.

Pretty, in a girl-next-door way, Zoe had a down-to-earth attraction that surprisingly appealed to Chase. She was as she appeared, there was no pretense with Zoe. Honest and earnest. A devoted mom. Charming. He shoved those thoughts aside. He didn't want to be charmed. He wanted to find out who had tried to kill her and her daughter.

"We'll be fine here," Liam said. "I can make a bed for Kylie on the floor with the couch cushions and a couple of blankets."

Zoe hesitated, the conflict of whether to leave Kylie or not was evident on her pretty face.

Chase didn't want to go. The idea of setting foot in a church sent ribbons of anxiety winding through him. After the loss of his family, he'd given up on God, angered that God had taken his family from him. "We can have the donations brought here."

He'd have one of the task force members head over to the church.

That he was willing to use government resources for his own agenda was a minor infraction, and he'd deal with whatever fallout came as long as it kept him from having to go.

"That won't be necessary," Zoe said, seeming to come to a decision. "I think Kylie will be just fine here with your dad. You and I can zip over and bring everything back. I'll need to go through it all to make sure I get the right sizes for us both. And we'll need to visit the bank so I can access my money and then stop at a store to get a few other things since I have to wait until the fire department releases my house. Though most everything will smell like smoke and be unsalvageable, not to mention the water damage." She shuddered and made a face. "At some point, I'll also need to go to the DMV since my purse with my ID was destroyed."

Zoe stood there with her expectant gaze holding his.

Chase's breath stalled. His heart jammed in his throat. He swallowed hard. She needed him to go with her. He couldn't deny her this. He didn't want to cause her more pain or disappointment because of his issues. He was going to have to suck it up and face God in His own house.

Zoe gripped the door handle of Chase's truck as he sped up. Blood pounded in her ears. "Is something wrong?"

"We're being followed," he said, his voice strained.

She twisted in her seat. Behind them, a white sedan drove so close she couldn't see the car's hood, let alone the license plate. Was the car trying to make them crash?

Without warning, Chase took a sharp turn, the truck tearing up the drive to the Elk Valley Community Church.

The sedan zoomed past the church parking lot entrance and raced down the street, turning left and disappearing out of sight.

"What was that about?" Zoe asked as Chase brought the truck to a halt in front of the church's main doors. Her heart rate was too fast, making her body shake.

"Not sure," Chase said. "But nothing good."

The grimness in his gaze had her on edge as they climbed from the vehicle and headed for the entrance to the church. The temperature was cool inside as Zoe stepped into the dark wood-paneled narthex. The smell of candle wax and furniture polish teased her nose. She realized Chase was literally dragging his feet behind her. Like an errant schoolboy unwilling to go to the principal's office.

Or was he still concerned about the sedan that had tailed them to the church?

He'd left Dash home to give Kylie and Liam extra protection. Plus, he'd called the Elk Valley Police Department to have a patrol car cruise the area. All in an effort to put her qualms at leaving Kylie behind at ease. Chase was a decent man who cared for her and Kylie. His thoughtfulness was appreciated.

Remembering how jaded he seemed, she was surprised he'd agreed to come with her to the church.

She pushed through the swinging doors to the sanctuary, letting the peace of God envelop her and settle her racing heart. She knew the church was just a building and God was with her always. But for some reason, she felt His presence more acutely when she was here. And she had to admit she also felt safe with Chase following behind her. There was no question in her mind, he wouldn't let anything happen to her. And she had to trust that Liam and Dash would protect Kylie.

Pastor Jerome came out of a room at the front of the sanctuary. A tall man with black curly hair and kind, dark eyes, he exuded a sense of well-being as he held out his hands for Zoe.

"Zoe, it's just terrible what happened," the pastor said, giving her hands a squeeze before releasing them. He turned his gaze to Chase, who came to stand beside Zoe. "Special Agent Rawlston. I didn't think we'd ever get you into our humble building."

"We're here about the donations for Zoe and Kylie." Chase said in a voice ripe with irritation.

Zoe frowned. She couldn't abide rudeness. "Yes, we are. And we are very grateful for the church's help." She gave Chase a pointed look.

Pastor Jerome's smile held understanding. "We have everything downstairs in our children's ministry room. This way." He turned and headed out a side door.

Chase moved to follow, and Zoe grabbed him by the elbow. "What is going on?"

She really wanted to understand him. Though she shouldn't give in to her curiosity. But there was something about him that tugged at her heart in a way no one else had. She needed to ignore it. Yet, the curiosity and the need to help him find peace were stronger than her need for self-preservation.

And that was nearly as terrifying as being in the crosshairs of a bomber.

FOUR

Chase pushed open the door leading to the staircase that would take them to the children's ministry area.

He stepped back to allow Zoe to enter first, grateful he had a reprieve from divulging the reasons behind his hesitation and his anger at God. He didn't want to discuss any of it. Especially not with Zoe.

His job was to keep Zoe safe. To do that he needed her to trust him. Knowing he'd failed to protect his own family wouldn't instill a lot of trust. He wouldn't be able to effectively protect her and little Kylie if she doubted him.

Guilt swamped Chase, making his chest tight. Rubbing at the spot over his heart where the pain lived, he took several breaths hoping to alleviate the pressure building inside of him.

Stay calm.

The image of the white sedan riding the truck's bumper had his fists clenching. It could have been nothing more than an over-aggressive driver. Or it could have been someone with a sinister agenda. If Chase hadn't turned into the church's drive, would the sedan have tried to run them off the road? Chase hadn't seen the license plate, but he made note of the make and model of the car.

As they descended the stairs to the basement area, Zoe said, "Please, know that you can talk to me. I'm a good listener."

"Sharing isn't part of the job," he said through clenched teeth.

They entered the area used for the children's ministries. The large space housed stacks of chairs in the corner. A drum set, guitar stand and piano sat in front of a picture window where light streamed into the room. In the center, several long tables had been set up. A mishmash of boxes and baby paraphernalia covered the tops and the floor. "Let's just get this done."

Zoe gave him a hard, censuring look before she pressed her lips together and focused her attention on the donations.

Chase stood by the exit doors, allowing Zoe and the pastor to pack several boxes with items she deemed appropriate.

"Thank you, Pastor Jerome," Zoe said as she stacked the boxes beside Chase. "These will be put to good use."

"I'm glad." Pastor Jerome smiled. "I'm sure more donations will be coming in over the next few days. Now that I know what you're needing, I'll take the liberty of putting those things aside and send the rest to a local charity."

"I'd appreciate it," Zoe said. She glanced at Chase and raised an eyebrow. "We can stop by again later this week, yes?"

Chase's smile was tight, the muscles of his face pulling as he said, "I'm sure we can make arrangements." He looked at the stack she'd made of boxes filled with clothes and toys and other baby paraphernalia. "Is this everything?"

"For now," she replied. "We'll have to make a couple of trips to your pickup."

"I'll bring the truck to this side entrance," Chase told her. "Pastor, can you stay with her for a few moments?"

Pastor Jerome nodded. "Of course."

Confident Zoe and the pastor would be safe for the time being, Chase hurried out of the building. He took a few deep breaths, easing the constricting band around his heart before heading to the front parking lot.

The hairs at his nape quivered. He paused, searching for the source of his sudden acute unease.

A white sedan, like the one that had trailed them to the church, idled at the end of the parking lot. The tinted windows kept him from seeing the driver. He headed for the car.

The sedan shot forward, the wheels squealing on the parking lot pavement and swerved, heading for the exit. Chase noted the plate number as the sedan drove out of the lot, turned the corner and disappeared from sight.

He'd run the plates when he returned to the station. He sent off a text to his team requesting they meet him in an hour.

Shaking off the disquiet and anger, he quickly drove his father's truck from the front parking lot to the rear side door. He, Zoe and the pastor loaded the boxes into the back bed in no time. Chase kept an alert eye out of any signs of the white sedan.

"Zoe, I understand you're heading up the reunion committee," the pastor said before they could climb into the vehicle.

Chase's gaze snapped to Zoe.

"I am," she affirmed.

Narrowing his gaze on the woman, Chase refrained from saying she'd neglected to tell him she was in charge of the reunion committee. A detail he needed to know.

"I hope the naysayers aren't getting you down," the pastor said. "This town needs some rejuvenation and healing. I plan to bring up the reunion at this coming Sunday's sermon. A last push to get people to sign up."

"I would appreciate that, Pastor," Zoe said. "Right now, we have a very sparse attendee list."

The pastor turned his gaze to Chase, "Will you be attending with Zoe for Sunday's service?"

Chase's heart thumped in his chest. Would Zoe insist on going? Probably. "Most likely." Would it be rude if he wore earplugs?

Zoe gave the pastor a hug. Chase held open the passenger door while Zoe climbed in.

Before he could start the engine, she put a hand on his arm. "Will you really come with me on Sunday?"

"I'm committed to protecting you," he said. "Where you go, I go."

She gave a satisfied smile. "Then we'll be going."

Biting back his reluctance, he started the

engine and drove toward home, while staying alert for any trouble. Namely a white sedan. "You didn't mention you were heading up the reunion committee."

She shrugged. "Is it relevant?"

"Everything is relevant unless I say it's not," he barked.

"Sorry." She tilted her head. "You're in a mood."

He took a deep breath, reining in the swirling emotions going into the church building had stirred. "For me to protect you, I need to know everything about your life. Including your involvement in this multigenerational reunion. The pastor said there are naysayers. I've heard rumblings, but I didn't realize the seriousness of the objections."

He'd had more pressing issues with the RMK. They'd theorized that maybe the announcement of the reunion had prodded the RMK out from under whatever rock he'd been hibernating beneath. "I need you to make a list of those who've opposed the reunion."

"I can do that." She turned away, keeping her face toward the window. "Though many of the negative comments have been posted on the reunion's social media page for everyone to see."

Chase regretted the harshness of his tone, but she didn't understand. An anxious flutter started low in his belly and worked through his chest, compelling him to say, "Look, God and I have not been on speaking terms for a long time."

She faced him. Her curious stare was a palpable force.

He slanted her a glance, noting the empathy on her face.

"Something happened," she said softly.

Understatement. "You could say that." He didn't want to talk about this. Not to her, not to anyone. But she would find out soon enough.

She'd see the pictures of Elsie and Tommy in the house. Zoe would wonder. Best to nip her curiosity in the bud now.

"I worked in DC as a field agent for the FBI for most of my career," he told her.

"Three years ago, Dash and I thwarted a bomb meant to blow up the National Art Gallery. The bomber escaped. Then he targeted me. Only he ended up killing my wife and two-year-old son." Pain lanced through his heart. "It should have been me, not them."

"Oh, Chase," she said with a breathy sigh of sympathy. Her soothing hand lay warm against his arm. "That's horrible."

He waited for the platitudes. For her to say he shouldn't blame God. That everything happened for a reason. All the things everyone else had said to him at the time when he was in the throes of grieving. Now, he endured the pitying glances and stares.

Instead, Zoe stayed silent, sitting with him in his misery.

And he was nearly brought to tears.

Zoe's heart ached for Chase and the tragedy he'd experienced. No wonder he was mad at God.

And he blamed himself.

He carried guilt like an anvil around his neck, thinking he should have died instead of his family. None of them should've died. It was devastating that life could unfold in such horrible ways. That evil could operate unchecked at times. But deep in her heart, she knew the tragedies of the world didn't negate God's sovereignty or His goodness.

But the knowing didn't make the pain hurt any less.

She couldn't fathom losing Kylie. Fear, dark and ugly, twisted in her gut. She sent up a plea for protection for her and Kylie, and peace for Chase.

The urge to hug him and offer some sort of comfort filled her, but she wasn't sure any gesture would be welcomed. Or that she should even make the gesture. Stepping over personal boundaries wouldn't be smart. She needed to keep an emotional as well as physical distance. Because anything resembling more than friendship would leave her open to heartache. She'd given a man her heart only to have him stomp on it. Better for her to not risk that sort of hurt again.

She settled for saying, "Thank you for sharing your past with me."

He gave a sharp nod as he pulled into the back parking lot of the Elk Valley police station. "I need that list of naysayers as soon as possible."

Tears clogged her throat despite her best effort to keep them at bay. He was hurting and grieving. There was nothing she could do to help him besides pray.

She didn't want to take on his pain. She had enough of her own. But how would she stay immune when they would be living under the same roof?

Chase tucked Zoe into the Elk Valley police chief's office. It was a comfortable space with a leather captain's chair behind the neatly organized desk. Two leather armchairs faced the desk. Zoe sat in one. She had pen and paper in hand to make a list of those in town who had expressed their opposition to having a multigenerational reunion.

As he headed to the conference room, he forced his mind to stay on task as he mulled over what Zoe had told him about the phone call right before the house exploded. A prank and unrelated? Or was the bomber making sure she was home and reveling in what was to come?

Most likely the latter.

"I assume you and your task force will be taking over the investigation into the bombing of Zoe Jenkins's home?" Police Chief Nora Quan asked as she fell into step with him. She was an impressive woman in her mid-fifties.

"I think we should work together," he said. "I hope you don't mind that I put Zoe in your office. I need to update my team."

"Not at all," Nora said.

Even though he had his boss's approval to use task force resources, he didn't want to overstep with Nora. "Zoe's the sister of one of the first victims. Our investigations intersect."

"Hey, I'm not complaining," Nora said, slanting him a glance beneath her dark bangs. "Just want to know what the expectations are. After an arsonist terrorized the town during the summer, the last thing we need is a bomber on the loose."

He couldn't agree more. Elk Valley had seen its fair share of tragedy and violence lately. They'd caught serial arsonist Bobby Linton last summer, who'd burned a path through town seeking revenge on people who'd wronged him in some way.

Now this morning's incident. Was this someone who felt wronged by Zoe? Her ex-husband? Or the RMK targeting the sister of one of his victims?

"The sooner we close this case and determine if the bomber is someone disgruntled by the reunion, or the RMK, the better," Nora continued. "If the bomber isn't the RMK, the reunion could be a powder keg that could bring the Rocky Mountain Killer back to town."

"Agreed." Chase stopped at the door of the conference room, where he'd arranged to meet the task force. They'd responded to the group text he'd sent. "I'll need extra patrols to help protect Zoe and her little girl."

Nora nodded. "Whatever you need. Tell the desk sergeant and he'll make it happen."

"Perfect." He didn't mention he'd already made the request before he and Zoe left the house.

Nora gave him a nod and headed down the hall, leaving Chase at the conference room entrance. He pulled open the door and the scent of freshly brewed coffee had him making a beeline to the coffee carafe. Several team members already sat at the conference table. Some of the K-9 handlers had their dogs at their feet while others, like Chase normally did, kept their dogs at their desks. Though being at the station without Dash was odd for Chase. Like he'd left an important piece of himself behind.

After pouring himself a cup, he settled into a seat at the head of the table. "How did the canvass go?"

Ashley leaned forward. Her dog, a male

black lab named Ozzy, rose to his haunches at her movement. She settled him with a hand to his neck. "We knocked on doors up and down the street. No one recalled seeing anything suspicious."

"We had several door camera videos sent to Isla," Rocco said, referring to the team's tech analyst, Isla Jimenez. Rocco's chocolate lab, who specialized in arson detection, lifted her head at the sound of her handler's voice.

"Good," Chase replied. "Hopefully, Isla will spot something we can use."

Isla was good at her job. And an asset to the team. One of his recruits. He hated that she had been hitting roadblocks in her attempt to adopt a toddler named Enzo. It wasn't right. He made a mental note to look into the situation personally. Things had escalated for Isla recently when an arsonist had set fire to her home—with her inside. Despite their initial thinking, it wasn't the work of the serial arsonist from last summer, but someone else. Someone who'd been messing with Isla and making life difficult for her over the last eight months. Now that Chase was back from Utah, he'd devote some time to investigating who had it out for her.

Turning his attention to the other important case the task force was working on, he asked the room at large, "Update on Evan Carr and Ryan York?"

Silence met his question. He raised an eyebrow.

Meadow, who'd left Grace, her female vizsla, kenneled at her desk, said, "We're still beating the bushes."

"Not the news I was hoping for," Chase said. "Any more sightings of Cowgirl?"

"Unfortunately, no," Bennett stated. He, too, had left his K-9 partner kenneled at his desk. "Thankfully, the puppies are healthy. Liana is working on potty training and is doing assessments to see if they will make good therapy dogs."

Liana Lightfoot, dog trainer extraordinaire, had been working with Cowgirl as a compassion K-9 before the dog's abduction. Chase had seen firsthand how devastated Liana had been when Cowgirl disappeared. He was confident in her ability to train Cowgirl's puppies.

Last month, while tracking the RMK in Utah, they'd discovered a crate full of puppies with a note from the killer. The words were etched in Chase's mind.

For the MCK9 Task Force. I can't easily elude you and care for them. But I'm keeping their mom, Killer. Oh, and Trevor Gage: you'll be dead soon enough.

Anger burned low in Chase's gut, tempered by the knowledge that the RMK held the lives of dogs in higher esteem than people. The RMK had renamed Cowgirl and had placed a pink sparkly collar on her according to the reports they'd received from witnesses.

Switching back to the new case, Chase said, "Regarding the bombing this morning, I've been given the green light for our team to take the lead on the investigation since Zoe Jenkins is in charge of the Elk Valley High reunion. We suspect that might have triggered the RMK to kill again. It's the tenth anniversary of the original murders." His gaze landed on each member of his team. "It's possible that the bombing isn't connected to the RMK. But I don't believe in coincidences. Zoe Jenkins was targeted for a reason."

"Are we operating with the thought that RMK is now targeting the families of the victims?" Meadow asked.

"It's a possibility. Until we know for sure, we should put the families on alert," Chase said. "But we have another possibility. Zoe is making a list of people who have expressed displeasure at the idea of the reunion. Ashley, Rocco, I want you to interview everyone on Zoe's list. And look at the reunion's social media. Apparently, there's been some negative comments. The incident today may have to do with the reunion and not the RMK."

"You think someone would be so against the reunion they'd try to kill Zoe and her kid?" Ian asked. "That's cold."

"People have done horrible things with less motive," Chase reminded them.

"Do you think the reunion committee members are in danger?" Rocco asked. "Sadie's on the committee." There was no mistaking the concern in his tone for his fiancée. Sadie Owens was a divorced mom with a three-year-old son named Myles. Rocco had been the one to protect Sadie and Myles when the serial arsonist—known locally as the Fire Man—had targeted them over the summer.

"I wouldn't think so unless they are connected to one of the victims in a crucial way," Chase assured him.

Rocco nodded, appearing deep in thought.

Chase was aware Sadie did have a connection to Aaron Anderson, one of the original victims. They'd dated briefly in high school, but Sadie's interviews with the task force last March, and her brevity of her time with Aaron, hadn't given the team the idea that she could be a suspect or a target.

Chase cleared his throat. "Zoe also received a phone call right before the explosion. Weird laughter. Sounded like a recording. No idea about gender." Chase looked at Meadow. "Can you have Isla run Zoe's phone records to see if we can find where the call originated?"

"Will do," Meadow said.

"Ian, would you do a deep dive into Zoe's ex-husband, Garrett Watson?" Chase asked. "Find out if he has an alibi for the time of the explosion."

"On it," Ian said.

Focusing on Bennett, Chase said, "Reach out to Ophelia and Kyle. See how quickly they can get here. I want Ophelia to take a look at the remnants of the bomb once the fire department releases the evidence."

Ophelia Clarke was a forensic specialist based in New Mexico. Recently, she helped on a case and Chase had been so impressed by her, he'd asked her to be on call with the task force and she'd happily agreed. Kyle West was a fellow FBI agent and K-9 handler from the New Mexico bureau. He was on the MCK9 task force and specialized in tracking serial killers with his partner, a male coonhound named

Rocky who specialized in cadaver detection. Kyle and Ophelia, his fiancée, were operating from Santa Fe.

"Got it," Bennett said. "I can also coordinate with the Elk Valley Fire Department. If the bomb was homemade, the perpetrator might have bought supplies in town. I can check the stores."

"Good idea." Chase pulled the task force laptop in front of him. He quickly did a DMV search on the license plate number of the sedan he'd seen in the church parking lot. Surprised, he sat back. The car was registered to Doctor Tyson Webb, Kylie's pediatrician. What was the doctor doing trailing them and then showing up at the church when they'd only just left him at the clinic?

"Boss?" Rocco said.

Giving himself a mental shake, he brought up a video chat screen and then sent a message to Hannah Scott, their team member providing protection to Trevor Gage.

His mind wandered back to the doctor.

There had to be a reasonable explanation as to why Tyson had been at the church in the middle of the day. Perhaps dropping off donations for Zoe and Kylie? But why follow them and then leave only to return? What was he playing at? "Bennett, could you check into the background of Doctor Tyson Webb?"

"Sure," Bennett said. "Something we should know?"

"Zoe and I stopped at the Elk Valley Community church on the way here. We were followed very closely by a white sedan." Chase told them. "Then later I saw the same car was in the parking lot. When I approached, the driver took off. It's probably nothing, but—"

"Better safe than sorry," Bennett finished.

A few minutes later, Hannah's face appeared on the laptop's video screen. Chase turned the computer so that Hannah had a view of the room while he sent the video stream to the large monitor attached to the conference room wall.

"Good morning, everyone," Hannah said, her bright green eyes sparkled.

A chorus of greetings followed. Chase cleared his throat, drawing everyone's attention. "Hannah, how are you and Trevor managing at the safe house?"

A man appeared over Hannah's shoulder. Trevor cocked an eyebrow. "We're fine."

Hannah made a face. "Antsy to get back to our lives."

Chase understood. Getting Trevor to go into hiding had taken Hannah almost being killed. But Chase would imagine sitting on the sidelines was hard for both of them. The idea that had surfaced earlier reared up again, half-formed. "Trevor, did you RSVP to the Elk Valley High multigenerational reunion?"

Trevor considered. "I might have. The invitation came last spring."

Chase's heart pounded. "I do think the reunion might have been the catalyst to prompt the RMK to kill again. The timing seems right."

"Makes sense," Rocco said. "The whole

town has been buzzing about the reunion for months."

"And causing some friction," Chase commented. "I hadn't realized how high the emotional meter was running. And if the reunion was the trigger for the RMK, we need to keep a close eye on the town. The RMK will strike when he's ready. It won't be obvious, and he'll try to catch us off guard."

"Do you think the RMK believes Trevor will return to Elk Valley?" Ashley asked.

"Maybe." Chase could use the idea of Trevor returning to town to trap the beast they called the RMK. Hmm. Chase needed to keep mulling over exactly how to execute the plan forming in his brain.

"Then the RMK could be here already," Meadow said.

Chase shrugged. "Not necessarily. At least not yet." He glanced at his watch. The timepiece brought both comfort and sorrow. It had been a gift from his late wife on their third anniversary. "I need to wrap this up. I'll let the others fill you in on what's happened. Rocco, Ashley, with me. Zoe should be done with that list."

Chase left the conference room with Rocco and Ashley at his heels. They entered the police chief's office.

Zoe rose and came around the desk to hand him the list. "I wrote as many names as I could remember."

"I'll take that." Ashley took the list and with a nod, she and Rocco left with the list in hand.

Chase noticed the dark circles bruising the tender skin beneath Zoe's eyes. She had to be exhausted. "Going to the bank and the DMV can wait until tomorrow. Let's head home."

Home. The word echoed through his head and his heart and landed with a thud in his gut. What had he done?

Chase lay on his bed with his head resting on his hands. The glow from the clock on the bedside table revealed the late hour. In the room next to his, baby Kylie fussed. Zoe's soft, soothing voice sang a lullaby.

Grief and guilt lay heavy on his heart as he listened.

The ding of an incoming text provided welcome relief. Glad for the distraction, he grabbed his phone. The number on the screen was unknown and held an attachment.

Wary, he opened the text.

A photo of Cowgirl, the pink collar with the word KILLER, sparkled around her neck. A man's hand and forearm, with the knife tattoo that they knew was on the arm of the Rocky Mountain Killer, held a copy of the *Elk Valley Daily Gazette* in the frame.

Chase sat up, the bed shifting beneath his weight. His heart pounded.

The local newspaper was from today.

FIVE

Unnerved by the image of the labradoodle, Cowgirl, with the local newspaper, Chase threw back the dark blue covers and sat on the edge of the bed just as another text came through from the same number.

Looking forward to the reunion and finishing what I started!

A coffin emoji followed the sentence.

Dread clamped around Chase's chest like a steel trap. He sent an alert to the team requesting a meeting first thing in the morning.

Having confirmation that the Rocky Mountain Killer was in Elk Valley caused anxiety to riot in Chase's gut.

Dash rose from his bed and came to sit beside Chase, resting his snout on his partner's knee.

"He's here," Chase whispered, placing a hand on his dog. Acid burned through his veins. It was time to end the serial killer's reign of terror once and for all.

Burying his fingers into the golden retriever's soft fur, Chase contemplated the killer's next move. What did he mean *finishing what I started*?

Was he referring to the bombing at Zoe's house?

There was no doubt the RMK was gunning for Trevor Gage. The killer had said as much in his previous messages. But Trevor was with Hannah, far away in a safe house, not here in Elk Valley.

Was there someone else the RMK planned to target? Who? When? Why?

The questions spun around his brain like a revolving door.

The inkling of the plan that had tickled Chase earlier blossomed. He would need to discuss with his team how best to orchestrate a trap for the Rocky Mountain Killer. But first, he needed his boss and the Elk Valley police chief to sign off on the concept that was bubbling inside his mind.

Since he wouldn't get any more sleep tonight, Chase dressed for the coming day and then leashed Dash. They paused outside Zoe and Kylie's room. The baby had finally settled down and all was quiet. Mother and daughter were safe and sound.

Chase intended to keep it that way.

Zoe awoke in the guestroom of Chase and Liam Rawlston's home. Kylie slept nearby in the donated crib. Morning sunlight flooded the room through the window that overlooked the well-groomed backyard.

The soft cream walls were decorated with seascape paintings and the soothing tones of the blue-and-green bed covering were comforting. She would never have imagined herself being here yesterday when she'd awakened at home.

So much had happened in a short time.

Her house had been blown up.

She and Kylie were now living in the Rawlston home for the foreseeable future, and she was grateful to the two men for their hospitality. She hoped Kylie's fussing in the middle of the night hadn't kept anyone else awake.

She couldn't stay here indefinitely. She needed to call her home insurance company and determine when she'd be able to rebuild her house. She mentally made a note to call the mayor and her other clients about their food orders, but she didn't have a plan yet. She'd have to figure out where she could resume working from. The stress of it all tightened the muscles in her shoulders.

While Kylie continued to sleep, Zoe took the opportunity to shower and change into a pair of jeans and a lightweight sweater she'd taken from the donation boxes.

She returned to a wide-awake baby. After changing Kylie's diaper, she dressed Kylie in a cute little pants and zip-up jacket ensemble in a peach color with a white onesie underneath. Socks with a ducky motif and a yellow bow for her hair completed the outfit.

Zoe carried Kylie out to the kitchen where she found Liam busy cooking pancakes and bacon. Chase was nowhere to be seen.

His dog, Dash, however, greeted her and Kylie with a wagging tail. The large plume swept through the air, stirring the scent of bacon and making Zoe's stomach rumble.

"I hope you're hungry," Liam said. "It's not often I get to make breakfast for more than just me."

"Chase doesn't eat breakfast?" she asked.

"Not often." Liam carried a stack of pancakes and a plate of bacon to the already set table. "He's usually up and gone before I'm awake."

A strange disappointment settled between her shoulders. "He's already gone?"

"He is," Liam said. He held up a sheet of paper. "He left a note."

From Liam's tone, Zoe guessed this was abnormal. She arched an eyebrow. "And?"

Liam grinned and read from the page. "Dad, watch over Zoe and Kylie. There's an officer stationed outside. I'll be back by lunch."

Even when absent, Chase was keeping her and Kylie safe. Warmth spread through Zoe. She glanced at the kitchen clock hanging over the sink. "I have to go to the bank and the DMV. Chase said we would do that today. I'd like to get it taken care of this morning. Kylie will need to go down for a nap around one."

Liam took his seat. "Dash and I will go with you. And we'll bring along Officer Eric Steve. I know his father."

"Great." She and Kylie should be safe with so much protection. "I also need to help the reunion committee pass out flyers." The stack that she'd had went up in flames. But she could get more from other committee members. She wouldn't let all the work fall on everyone else without doing her share.

"Then it's a plan." Liam forked a pancake and waved it in the air. "Will the baby eat one?"

"She loves pancakes," Zoe assured him. Her heart filled with gratitude for these kind people. But deep inside, she feared this lull wouldn't last. How much longer would she have to look over her shoulder to make sure no one was coming after her and Kylie again?

The early morning meeting with the team broke up just after eight o'clock. The shock of seeing Cowgirl and realizing that the Rocky Mountain Killer had indeed arrived back in Elk Valley had everyone on high alert.

"We don't want to cause a panic with the public," Chase told his team. "For now, keep the news to yourselves. We will continue investigating yesterday's bombing of the Jenkins house while working to locate the RMK. If you see anything suspicious, don't hesitate to call for backup. I'd rather we overreact than miss our opportunity to catch the RMK."

"I'll see if I can enhance this photo of Cowgirl and the newspaper to figure out where it was taken," tech analyst Isla Jimenez said.

Chase nodded. "Perfect."

"I've been combing through the nasty comments on the reunion's social media pages," Meadow said. "There are some very disgruntled people out there."

"Tell me about it," Ashley said. She gestured to Rocco. "We interviewed four names on Zoe's list yesterday. Each one gave us an earful about how they didn't approve of the event while the Rocky Mountain Killer was still on the loose. Most find the event in poor taste while some fear it will draw the RMK back. Which I have to say is a legit concern."

"Yes we've established the reunion's connection to the RMK," Chase said.

"A few of the real nasty social media comments are by one poster," Meadow said. "Isla and I are working to find the ISP and the name of the person behind it."

Rocco spread his hands on the conference room table. "Despite my misgivings, which I've expressed to Sadie, the committee members are moving forward with the reunion."

Which was exactly what Chase would need for his plan to work.

"Boss, I checked into Dr. Webb," Bennett said. "Squeaky clean. Not even a parking ticket. He was with a patient when I called. He hasn't called back yet. I'll follow up later today."

"Thank you," Chase said. "Let me know what you find out. Does anyone have an ETA on Ophelia and Kyle?"

"They should be here this afternoon," Ashley offered.

"Good." He needed the evidence from Zoe's house examined, and he wanted Ophelia's close eye on it. He'd arranged to have her come out with Kyle to work the case.

He considered bringing in Idaho Deputy Sheriff Selena Smith, but she was investigating in Utah and would jump in as backup for Hannah if need be should the RMK show up there looking for Trevor.

After dismissing the meeting, Chase headed to the police chief's office. An hour ago, he'd requested a meeting with Nora Quan, and his boss at the FBI Special Agent in Charge Cara Haines, who would call in from DC. Both were waiting when he arrived. He broke the news that the Rocky Mountain Killer was in Elk Valley.

Nora stared at the photo the RMK had texted him. "Unbelievable."

"Send me a copy," Cara said, her voice tinny over the speakerphone.

Taking his phone back from Nora, he forwarded the image to Cara. Then he ran his idea for trapping RMK by the two women.

"So let me get this straight," Cara said, the intensity of her tone clear through the speaker. "You intend to go around town telling everyone that Trevor Gage has returned for the reunion."

"Correct," Chase said. "I'll rent a vacation house in his name." Trevor's family ranch had long been sold and the family relocated after the first three murders. "And I'll drive a truck around with his company logo on the side."

"So, in other words, you're going to be the bait," Nora said. She stood behind her desk with her arms folded over her perfectly tailored pantsuit.

"Exactly." To Chase it made perfect sense. He would pose as Trevor and hope the RMK made a move on him. He needed their approval before he presented the plan to the team. "It'll lure one of our suspects out. My inclination is to say Ryan York is our culprit because he's the only one with a registered handgun that could match the bullets taken from the victims." They'd also never been able to pin York down for an interview. He'd moved out of state years ago and tracking his whereabouts had been impossible. Elusive like the RMK. Because they were one and the same?

"We all know, bad guys can get their

hands on a weapon without going through the process of registering it," Nora pointed out.

"True," Chase conceded.

"And if the RMK comes after you while you're posing as Trevor," Cara said, "you and the team will be ready to take him down? Whether the suspect turns out to be Ryan York or Evan Carr or someone else."

"Yes," Chase confirmed. "Once we get everything all situated, between the task force, Elk Valley PD and the US marshals service, we can't fail. The plan will work."

It had to.

"Assuming the RMK doesn't get wind of the plan," Nora said. "You forget, Chase, this is a small town. Gossip flows down Main Street like rainwater down a gutter."

"That's what I'm counting on," Chase said. "All we have to do is tell a couple of people that Trevor Gage RSVP'd and he's returning to Elk Valley for the reunion. The wagging tongues of this town will do the rest to lure the RMK into the trap."

"What about Zoe Jenkins and her baby?" Nora asked.

"We're working on figuring out who planted the bomb at her house and why," he told her.

"The RMK?" Cara asked.

"Maybe," Chase replied with doubt evident in his tone. "The only issue is that the use of an incendiary device deviates from the RMK's usual modus operandi."

"Criminals have been known to change tactics," Cara reminded him. "The RMK included."

"Agreed." The first three victims of the Rocky Mountain Killer had been shot in the chest. The last three more recent victims had also been shot in the chest, but the RMK had added a knife buried in two of his victims' chests with a note taunting the police. In Utah, when Trevor Gage had been within reach, the RMK had opened fire and given chase through the woods to hunt Gage down—a departure from his usual MO of killing his victims in a barn. Still, changing from shooting to bombing was a big shift. "The RMK has proven to be unpredictable."

"Everyone in town knows Ms. Jenkins is staying with you and your dad," Nora told him.

Chase sighed. "I'm aware. My dad, Dash and a patrolman are keeping watch over Zoe and Kylie. I will also have one of the task force members stay with her when I'm posing as Trevor." Though Chase knew none of his team would want to be sidelined from the action of taking down the Rocky Mountain Killer, it couldn't be helped. "Hopefully, long before this plan comes to fruition, we will have uncovered who targeted Zoe and her baby."

"Do you have any suspects besides the RMK?" Nora asked.

"We are looking into her ex-husband. Apparently, the divorce was not amicable," Chase told the women. "Also there have been many in town opposed to this upcoming reunion. We are looking into all those who have expressed a negative response."

Nora narrowed her gaze behind her

glasses. "I don't like the idea of one of our townspeople trying to solve their problems so horrifically."

"Nor do I," Chase said. "Once our team's crime scene investigator arrives and can look at the evidence, we'll know more."

Nora rose from her desk. "Keep me informed. Cara, it was nice to meet you via the phone. We will have to get together in real life one day."

"Same here," Cara said. "Chase, keep me in the loop."

"One moment." Chase held up a hand. "Just so I have clarity, you both approve of my plan to trap the RMK?"

Nora gave a slow nod. "Yes. Let us know how we can help."

Cara's sigh came through the line. "You have permission. Keep Sully in the loop. If this goes sideways, Chase…it just better not." With that, his boss hung up.

Nora chuckled. "I like her." She made a shooing motion with her hand at Chase. "Go do what you need to do."

Chase saluted Nora and walked out of the

conference room, satisfied to have a plan of action in place. Drawing out the Rocky Mountain Killer meant Chase needed to be prepared for a final showdown. One way or another, justice would prevail.

Zoe pushed Kylie in a donated stroller along the sidewalk of Elk Valley Park with Liam holding on to Dash's leash and a patrol officer, Eric Steve, following close behind. The park was located across the street from town hall. The reunion committee had voted to hold the reunion in the event ballroom of the town hall building.

With less than a week to go before the big event, pressure to get everything done built inside Zoe's chest. The committee needed to decorate the ballroom at least a few days ahead of time. Zoe and Sadie Owens had partnered to cater the event, with Sadie providing a mix of Italian fare and subs, while Zoe had planned some dishes for those with dietary restrictions. Though now, Zoe wondered where she was going to prepare the food. She really needed to find a place.

She'd lost not only her home and all her belongings, but her business would now suffer until she could make other arrangements. It wasn't fair. Why had someone done something so awful? What had they hoped to gain by killing her?

Glancing sideways at Liam, who'd moved up with Dash and now sauntered beside the stroller, Zoe contemplated asking if she could borrow the man's kitchen. But that would be a big ask. Liam was so kind and generous, and she appreciated all he and Chase were doing for her and Kylie. She didn't want to overstep and take advantage of their hospitality. Besides, she needed to think of a long-term solution until her house was fixed and livable again. No, it would be better to ask Sadie to use her catering company's kitchen.

With that thought in mind, she said, "Would you mind if we stop at Sadie's Subs?"

"I love their sandwiches," Liam said and shifted direction.

Zoe aimed the stroller toward the pink-flowered food truck parked at the end of the park's lot.

Sadie waved from inside the food truck window. A moment later, she exited the truck and hurried to hug Zoe.

Sadie's pale blonde hair was twisted up in a bun secured beneath a hairnet. Her big, luminous green eyes searched Zoe's. "I've been so worried about you," she said. "Rocco told me what happened. Is there anything I can do to help?"

"As a matter of fact, a couple of things," Zoe said. "Since I no longer have a kitchen… could I use yours for the reunion?"

Nodding eagerly, Sadie said, "Yes, of course."

Relieved to have that problem solved, Zoe said, "I was hoping you have some extra reunion flyers I could pass out."

"Don't worry about those," Sadie said. "The rest of the reunion committee can take care of it." Sadie winked. "I tuck one into every order."

Zoe laughed. "Well, that is one way to spread the word."

Sadie shifted her focus to the men with Zoe. "Can I get you folks anything to eat?"

Liam patted his stomach. "We had a good breakfast. But I might take an Italian sub for later?"

"You got it. I'll make enough for you all to have some." Sadie hurried back to her food truck.

"Oh, here comes trouble," Liam said, though there was a definite lift to his voice.

Zoe followed his gaze to an older woman with graying hair and a flowing outfit that made her look like she was floating rather than walking. Martha Baldwin, Jessie's grandmother, made a beeline for Zoe.

"Well, hello there," Martha said. "Jessie told me she saw you at the Rusty Spoke yesterday." Martha air-kissed Zoe and then bent down to place a kiss on Kylie's forehead. She straightened and smile at Liam.

"Hello, Liam. Nice to see you out and about." She smiled at the officer.

"Nice to see you, Martha." Liam's smile was wide and genuine. "You're always a ray of sunshine."

Pink defined the contours of Martha's cheeks. "You're always the charmer."

"I say it like I see it," Liam retorted with a wink.

Martha shook her head as she moved away into the park.

Zoe had watched the exchange between the two and suppressed a giggle at their flirtation.

Sadie rejoined them and handed Liam a bag. "Italian subs for everyone. I threw in an extra one for Chase."

"What do I owe you?" Liam reached for his wallet.

"On the house," Sadie said with a wave of her hand. Turning her attention to Zoe, Sadie asked, "Are we still on for our reunion committee meeting later this week?"

"We sure are." Zoe was determined to make the reunion a success. Seth would have liked the idea of everyone gathering; he'd always been up for a party. He'd had a playful side that at times turned sour when he was trying to impress his friends. He'd craved attention. Any attention. Good or bad. Seth had had his issues, but he hadn't deserved being murdered. "I'm not going to let anybody prevent us from putting on this reunion."

"We'll see about that," a deep male voice said from behind Zoe. She startled and whirled around to find herself nose to chest with Chase.

"Excuse me?" Her knee-jerk reaction was a defensive outage. Garrett had been tyrannical, thinking he had the right to boss her around. She hadn't realized how deeply his autocratic behavior had eroded away her self-esteem until he had abandoned her and Kylie. She had vowed never again to be controlled by someone else.

"We need to find out who destroyed your home and why, first," Chase said. "And I would prefer if you weren't out roaming around town making a target of yourself."

Taking Dash's leash, Chase turned to glare at his father. "What part of my note did you not get?"

Zoe pushed Kylie's stroller in between Chase and his father. "Your father, Dash and Officer Steve accompanied me to the bank and the DMV. I hardly think that counts as making a target of myself."

Chase ran a hand through his hair. A mix of emotions marched across his face. "Maybe not knowingly. I need you and Kylie to be safe."

Her heart fluttered as she recalled what had happened to his wife and child. She hadn't thought about how protecting her and Kylie would affect him. She'd only thought of her own agenda and not the pain he was carrying around. She didn't want to care, but she did. "I'm sorry we worried you."

Chase gave her a nod and then heaved out a heavy breath. "Are we ready to return to the house?"

Liam held up the bag Sadie had given him. "Lunch for us all." Liam and the patrol officer walked on ahead as Sadie said her goodbyes and returned to her truck.

Still holding on to Dash's leash, Chase placed his hands on the stroller's handle. "I've got this."

Surprised and oddly delighted, Zoe released her hold and let him escort them across the parking lot toward the street corner where they'd cross and head back to his house.

The rev of an engine cut through the air, the loud sound making Zoe wince. The screech of tires spinning on the asphalt made her shudder. She turned her head in time to see a white sedan bolt out of a parking space. The front end of the car was aimed straight at them.

SIX

In the space of a heartbeat, Chase assessed the threat as the white sedan ate up the space between its front end and Zoe and Kylie. Clearly, the driver intended to mow them down.

Reacting with a jolt of adrenaline, Chase released his hold on Dash's leash, certain the dog would jump out of the way.

"Dad!" Chase gave the stroller a mighty shove, pushing it into his father's hands. As soon as Chase let go of the stroller, he hooked an arm around Zoe, drew her body up tight against his and dove out of the way. At the last second, he twisted to land on his right shoulder and hip, while Zoe's body landed on top of him, knocking the wind from his lungs.

The car zipped past them with only a few inches of clearance before making a sharp turn and gunning it out of the parking lot exit.

Thankfully, Chase had tucked his chin so his head hadn't bounced off the asphalt. But he hadn't been able to see the driver either.

Zoe curled into Chase's chest. Her body shook. No doubt from shock.

He tightened his hold, running a soothing hand down her back. People gathered around them.

Officer Steve crouched down next to Chase. "Are you okay, sir?"

"We will be," Chase told the man as he rolled onto his backside, lifting Zoe with him as he sat up. "Zoe, you're okay. I've got you."

She lifted her head, her brown hair shielding her face. "Kylie!"

"Safe. Over here," Liam called out. He snuggled Kylie to his chest.

Zoe melted against him. "That was close."

"Too close," Chase murmured and

smoothed back her hair to reveal her fear-filled eyes.

"By the grace of God, you managed to save both Kylie and me," Zoe said.

Seething that he hadn't seen the threat, Chase grunted. He chose not to think too closely about God's hand in the situation. Right now, he just wanted to know who was driving that car. "Did anyone see the driver?"

"The tinting on the windows was too dark," the police officer said. "But I'll put a BOLO out on it."

Chase didn't need the "be on the look-out" for the sedan. "I know who it belongs to," Chase told the officer.

Zoe pushed away from his chest and scrambled out of his arms. She faced him in a crouch, her eyes wide and luminous. "Whose car is it?"

"Dr. Webb's."

Zoe frowned and shook her head. "That doesn't make any sense."

She rose to her feet and hurried over to where Kylie and Liam waited. Zoe took possession of her daughter, kissing her cheeks and hugging her close.

Getting to his feet, Chase ignored the pain sloshing through the various spots where he'd landed on his right side. He'd take an Epsom salt bath tonight. That was par for the course in law enforcement. You took your lumps. Figuratively and literally.

Sadie rushed forward to wrap her arms around Zoe. "Oh my! I nearly had a heart attack. Are you hurt?"

"Chase took the brunt of the landing," Zoe said, her gaze searching his.

Dash moved to lean against Chase's leg.

"Son, are you okay?" Liam put his hand on Chase's shoulder.

"I'm fine." Chase held up a hand, stalling anyone from further questions and commiseration. "We need to get back to the house now."

Picking up Dash's leash, Chase tried not to limp from the ache in his hip as he hustled Zoe, Kylie and his dad down Main Street with Officer Steve close on their heels. They quickly turn down the residential street where they lived. Chase kept an alert eye out for the white sedan. As soon as they reached the house and were safely inside, Chase called Bennett.

"Hey, boss," Bennett said by way of greeting.

"Bring Dr. Webb in for questioning," Chase said in a hard tone.

"Did something else happen?"

"He just tried to run down Zoe and Kylie," he said.

"On it," Bennett said and hung up without preamble.

Chase then dialed Ashley's number. When the officer answered, Chase said, "Is Dr. Tyson Webb on that list of names of people who don't think the reunion should happen?"

"Well, hello to you, too," Ashley said. "Let me look."

Chase winced. He didn't have time for pleasantries right now. He had to know who had just tried to run down Zoe and Kylie. It wasn't lost on him that he'd been in the path of the car, as well.

"Nope," Ashley said. "Is everything okay, boss?"

"Not really." He told her about the incident.

"Could it have been the RMK?" Concern ran through her tone.

Chase considered this. "The RMK likes to look his victims in the eye when he shoots them. I can't see him using a car. It's too impersonal."

"So is a bombing."

Chase couldn't deny that fact. The RMK didn't want anyone to recognize him. Chase wished they had a bead on Ryan York. Evan Carr's place outside of town was being watched but so far he hadn't shown.

"I'll keep digging through the names Zoe gave, but so far, I can't point to a suspect among them," Ashley stated. "Everyone has been very cooperative though vocal in their displeasure."

"You can't discount anyone at this point," Chase told her. "Some of the most innocent appearing and friendly people are monsters in disguise."

"Yes, sir."

Chase hung up with Ashley and called Meadow. She answered on the second ring. "Boss, I was just going to call you."

"Tell me," Chase said.

"We uncovered our most malicious poster on the reunion's social media pages," Meadow said. "Garrett Watson. Zoe's ex-husband."

Chase gritted his teeth and anger let loose a sharp spear through him. "Have Rocco and Ian bring him in. I'll be at headquarters in an hour."

"Will do. But it will take more than an hour," Meadow said. "Garrett now lives in Jackson Hole."

Chase hung up and entered the kitchen where his dad was handing out the Italian sub sandwiches. Unsure he could eat, but also aware he needed to, Chase accepted a wrapped sandwich. Liam then walked outside to give Officer Steve a sub.

Being in pain on an empty stomach wasn't

a good idea. The salt bath would have to wait. For now, Chase swallowed two over-the-counter pain relievers with a glass of water and then dug into his Italian sub.

Zoe reached over from her place at the table and laid her small, delicate hand on his forearm. "Thank you, again. If you hadn't thought so quickly..."

He stared at her hand on his arm, liking the way warmth traveled through his system. Then he glanced up, meeting her equally warm gaze. "I'm just glad I was there to protect you."

Because he hadn't been there to protect his wife and son.

Deep in Zoe's brown eyes, he saw her understanding. She squeezed his arm. "I'm glad you were, too."

His heart contracted in his chest. Her words soothed the ache of grief and guilt biting through him. He jerked his gaze away from her and lifted the sandwich to his mouth, forcing her to release her hold on him. He couldn't let her become at-

tached to him. Nor could he become attached to her.

He wouldn't be able to survive another
loss.

Zoe pushed the sting of rejection away.
There was no reason for her to feel slighted
that Chase practically shook her hand off
his arm. She shouldn't be touching him
anyway. The last thing she wanted was
for him to get the wrong idea and think
she was looking for a deeper relationship.

He had to be so frustrated with her and
the situation. She didn't understand why he
didn't assign someone else to her protection. But she certainly wouldn't voice the
thought, because she had no doubt that she
and Kylie were safe with Chase and his father and the big, beautiful golden retriever.

Reaching over to give Kylie a piece of
banana, Chase asked, "What's Garrett
doing in Jackson Hole?"

The question jarred Zoe. "He moved
there after the divorce and opened another
Watson Motors."

"Does Garrett have any connection to Dr. Webb?"

Did Chase think Garrett had been driving the vehicle that had tried to run them over? Zoe shook her head. "Garrett was not behind the wheel of that car."

"We don't know that for sure," Chase said, his tone razor-sharp even as he let Kylie wrap her chubby fingers around his index finger. "What we do know is that Garrett Watson is one of the offensive posters on the reunion page's social media."

Zoe tucked in her chin as her mind grappled with this news. Kylie giggled as Chase blew a raspberry on her hand. "I looked through those posts. I didn't see his name or his email address."

"Of course, you didn't," Chase told her. "He has a separate email for his vitriol. But my tech analyst tracked down the ISP, and it belongs to your husband."

"Ex-husband," she clarified with her own growing irritation. "I can't imagine why he would be so negative. When I brought up the concept of a reunion before we found out I was pregnant, he thought it was a good idea. He agreed with me that the town needed to heal and a multigenerational reunion would be a perfect way for everyone to come together and remember we are all still alive."

Chase pierced her with his intense dark gaze over Kylie's head. "When was the last time you saw or heard from Evan Carr? Or Ryan York?"

Surprise washed over her. Of course, Zoe knew who the two men were. Though to be honest, she still thought of them as boys because the last time she'd seen either one had been when they'd graduated from high school a few years ahead of her. "I can tell you neither one has RSVP'd for the reunion. Other than that, it's been over a decade since I've seen either of them."

"Was Seth friends with Evan or Ryan?"

"I don't recall them being friends. Seth had dated Ryan's sister, Shelly," she said. Sadness camped out in her chest. "I know people, Ryan in particular, blamed Seth for Shelly's death."

"Did Ryan ever confront Seth?"

"Yes," she replied, remembering that day and the horrible scene. "Ryan came to the house, enraged, and yelled at Seth for pushing his sister into committing suicide. My parents had to threaten to call the police before Ryan would leave."

Chase's eyebrows shot up. "They didn't report the altercation?"

"Not that I know of." She shook her head. "Seth was wild as a teen. Always getting into trouble. Seeking attention. My parents shielded me from his antics as best they could. My poor parents didn't have any idea how to handle my brother."

Why was he asking these questions?

A horrifying thought ran through her brain, sending a chill down her spine. "Do you think Ryan is the Rocky Mountain Killer?"

"I can't divulge information on an ongoing case," Chase said. "Was Ryan or Evan friends with Garrett?"

She had to think hard about that. "Honestly, I don't know," she said. "I don't know who Garrett's friends were in high school. You'd know better than me since you were closer to his age. He never mentioned Ryan or Evan while we were married."

Kylie fussed in the highchair, banging her hands on the tray, a clear indication she wanted out. Zoe balled up her sandwich wrapper.

"I'll take that," Chase said, holding out his hand.

With a grateful smile, she dropped the crumpled wrapper into his palm. "Kylie and I are going to take a nap. It's been a stressful twenty-four hours."

The tenderness on Chase's face squeezed her heart. "Dad and Dash will be here, along with Officer Steve. Please don't leave again without letting me know."

Her first instinct was to rebel and tell him she didn't need his permission to do anything, but then she reined in her ego and nodded her acquiescence. "We'll do that. Thank you again, Chase."

She lifted Kylie out of the high chair and turned to head toward the hallway just as Chase stood up, blocking her path.

He ran a knuckle down Kylie's cheek. "She's such a sweetie."

Kylie's little fingers wrapped around his finger again.

"She likes you," Zoe said. "You're good with her. You made her giggle. That's a sign she trusts you."

"My son, Tommy, had the best laugh," he said, his eyes misting as he lifted Kylie's hand and kissed her knuckles.

Empathy for his loss constricted her throat but she managed to say, "I'm sure you miss him."

Seeming to pull himself together, Chase said in a soft voice, "Rest well, little one."

Prying Kylie's fingers away from Chase, Zoe stared into his eyes. An unbidden thought ran through her brain.

Chase would have been—would be—a really good dad. She hated that he'd been robbed of his family by the senseless and destructive actions of someone else. She wanted to help him heal from the pain. But to do that she would have to open her heart. She couldn't let down her defenses around Chase. She wouldn't take the risk of being hurt again.

As soon as it was safe, they'd go their separate ways.

After giving instructions to his father and Officer Steve to make sure that Zoe and Kylie remained inside for the rest of the day, Chase walked from the house to the police station. He needed a few moments to catch his breath and clear his mind of a pair of sweet brown eyes and the soft soothing tone of Zoe singing to baby Kylie as she put the little girl down for a nap. He couldn't help but hear as he'd changed out of his dirt-smeared clothes into fresh slacks and a dark blue long-sleeve collared shirt with the MCK9 logo on the breast pocket.

Zoe was a good mom. There was no mistaking her love for Kylie. He saw her bristle a time or two whenever he had given her instructions. He wondered about that. Wondered what hurts she carried from her marriage. From the death of her brother. Chase had left town before Seth had entered high school. So he had no recollection of him. But from all accounts, Seth had been a troublemaker. Zoe had mentioned her parents had difficulties with their son. He could imagine it had been hard for Zoe living under the cloud of her brother's less-than-stellar behavior. His heart ached for her.

When Chase entered the police station, Ashley was bouncing on her heels, waiting for him. "You are not going to believe what I just found out."

Falling in step with her as they headed to the conference room, he said, "Lay it on me."

"Melissa, you know, my new sister-in-law?" Ashley said.

"I'm aware that you have a new sister-in-law," he told her. Ashley and Cade Mc-Neal had married not long ago after a case where Cade's sister, Melissa, and her son were in jeopardy.

A flush stained Ashley's cheeks. "Right. Anyway, Melissa works at the Rusty Spoke with Jessie Baldwin—"

"Again, I'm aware." This time he couldn't keep the impatience from his tone.

Ashley grimaced. "Melissa and Jessie were talking with Jessie's grandma, Martha Baldwin, who heard from Teresa Newton that her granddaughter had been secretly engaged to Brad Kingsley before his death." She said the last part in a rush as if the excitement was too much to contain.

Chase stopped at the door to the conference room. He cocked his head as he digested her words. "Brad Kingsley was secretly engaged to someone? Why didn't we know this?" Brad was one of the RMK's initial victims. And his fiancée hadn't come up when they'd interviewed locals connected to the cold cases back in March.

"According to Martha, Teresa said that her granddaughter was distraught when

Brad was killed, and her parents feared for her safety. They moved away a month later."

Chase's hand tightened on the conference room door handle. "And does this mysterious fiancée have a name?"

"Haley Newton."

The name conjured up a woman in scrubs. "She's a nurse at the Elk Valley Community Hospital."

Ashley nodded. "She is. She returned to Elk Valley a few years ago."

"Bring her in for questioning," Chase said, his tone sharper than he intended.

"Going to do that now," Ashley said and hurried away.

Chase frowned, not liking how he'd handle that situation. His blood was running too hot from the close call with Zoe and Kylie. He didn't need to be taking it out on his team.

He entered the conference room and found crime scene investigators Ophelia and Kyle, along with Meadow.

"Good to see you two," Chase said.

"Ophelia, I need you to get over to the FD and sift through the bombing residue collected at Zoe's house. I want to know everything you can find out about the bomber."

"Sorry we couldn't get here sooner," Kyle said. "Ophelia needed to get permission from her boss to take a few days off to help the team and we had to arrange for childcare for my nephew."

He understood the childcare dilemmas of his team. "You're here now. That's all that matters," Chase said. He'd never ask the team to put duties before arranging childcare. Ashley and her fiancé, Cade, helped with their nephew's care. Bennett and Naomi had just welcomed a brand-new baby boy. Isla was trying to adopt a child. Now Chase had a baby living in his house, along with her beautiful mother. Why did his thoughts always return to Zoe?

He gave himself a mental shake. *Stay on task*, he admonished himself.

Bennett pushed open the door to the conference room, "I have Dr. Webb sitting in interrogation room one."

Chase followed Bennett to the interrogation room and walked inside. The doctor sat in a hard plastic chair at the lone table sitting in the middle of the room.

Dr. Webb smiled. "Special Agent Rawlston. How is Kylie? And Zoe?"

Interesting he'd asked about the pair so quickly. Taking the seat across from him, Chase said, "They're safe."

The doctor nodded. "Good to know. My wife and I've been praying for them."

Chase sent Bennett a questioning look. Bennett nodded, confirming the doctor was married.

Maybe they needed to investigate the doctor's wife, too. Was this a case of the doctor becoming too friendly with a patient and a jealous wife? Chase placed his hands on the table. "Tell me about your relationship with Zoe Jenkins?"

Dr. Webb cocked his head. "I'm her daughter's pediatrician."

"Is that all?" Chase persisted.

"I'm not sure what you're getting at here, Agent Rawlston, but I do not appreciate the insinuation that I would have less than a professional relationship with one of the parents of my patient."

His indignation rang true. "Where were you yesterday afternoon?"

"Seeing patients," the doctor said. "In fact, I saw Kylie and Zoe and you at the hospital."

"What about after seeing Zoe and Kylie? Were you at the Elk Valley Christian Church?"

Dr. Webb shook his head. "No, I had patients until well after six p.m. What is this all about?"

"Where were you this morning?"

The doctor heaved an exasperated sigh. "Seeing patients. I am a doctor. That is what I do."

"Why was your white sedan seen at the church yesterday afternoon?"

Frowning, Dr. Webb said, "That's what this is about? My car? Don't you people talk to each other? I reported my car stolen last evening when I was leaving the hospital."

Chase arched an eyebrow and glanced at Bennett. Bennett made a face and ducked out the door. Irritation swamped Chase. This was his fault. If he'd allowed Officer Steve to put the BOLO out on the sedan, he would have known it had been reported stolen. "While my colleague checks on that report, I'd like a list of the patients you've seen in the past twenty-four hours."

"You know I can't do that." Dr. Webb said. "HIPPA laws and all."

"Then I will get a court order asking for the records of everyone you've seen."

"Is this really necessary?" Dr. Webb said. "When your colleague comes back, he will tell you I did indeed report my car stolen. My wife drove me to work this morning. I've not left the hospital until your man there picked me up and brought me here."

"We'll check the hospital CCTV to confirm your statement," Chase said.

Bennett opened the door with a contrite

pinch to his expression. "The white sedan was indeed reported stolen last night."

Chase stood, softening his expression. "We thank you for your cooperation, Dr. Webb. I'm sure the police department will find your car soon. We will verify that you were at the hospital, but you're free to leave for now."

Dr. Webb stood and held out his hand.

Surprised, Chase shook the man's hand.

"No hard feelings, Agent Rawlston," Dr. Webb said, releasing his hold on Chase. "I know you're just doing your job. Whatever you need to do to keep Zoe and Kylie safe, I approve of. Now, if your man could give me a ride back to the hospital?"

Bennett held the door wider. "This way, Doc."

Chase rubbed his temples. The over-the-counter pain meds were wearing off. His shoulder was throbbing and his hip protested after sitting on the hard chair.

He headed into the kitchen for an ice pack, a bottle of water and some more medication.

Rocco appeared around the corner of the hallway with Garrett Watson in tow. Chase pivoted away from the kitchen and followed Rocco and Garrett to the same interrogation room they had just occupied with Dr. Webb.

It was going to be a long day.

SEVEN

Chase watched as Rocco led Garrett Watson into the interrogation room. Tall with a wide chest, Zoe's ex-husband carried himself with an arrogant swagger that grated on Chase's nerves.

This was the man who'd won Zoe's heart and then tossed it away.

Rocco stepped out of the interrogation room, shutting Watson inside.

"I thought he was living in Jackson Hole," Chase commented.

"He is," Rocco said. "He was halfway to Elk Valley when I reached him by phone. I met him on the outskirts of town and escorted him here."

Interesting. Suspicious? To be determined.

"Why was he coming to Elk Valley?"

"He'd heard about the explosion at his ex-wife's house," Rocco said. "Claims he was coming to make sure they were okay."

Chase wasn't sure what to think of that information. The man abandoned his family and now rushed to check on them? To make sure they were safe, or to finish what he'd started?

Carrying the file with the information Meadow and Isla had gathered, he opened the door to the interrogation room and stepped inside with Rocco close behind him.

Garrett Watson sat at the table in the same place that Dr. Webb had just vacated.

Chase tried to view Garrett dispassionately, but all he could think about was that this man had deserted his wife and child, leaving them alone and unprotected. Garrett had had the most precious thing in life—a family—and he threw it away. It infuriated Chase to no end.

Corralling his thoughts, he grabbed the chair opposite Garrett and dragged it away from the table, letting the legs scrape along the concrete floor with an unnerving noise that visibly shuddered through Garrett.

Once he had the chair situated at a comfortable distance from the table, Chase sat. "Thank you, Garrett, for coming in. I understand you were headed to Elk Valley to check on Zoe and Kylie."

"Yes. I'd like to see my wife and daughter," Garrett said. "I don't understand why you wanted to see me."

"Ex-wife," Chase clarified much the way Zoe had clarified the status of her relationship to Garrett earlier that day. "You're here because I want to know what type of explosives you used to blow up your ex-wife's house."

Chase watched Garrett closely.

The man's eyes widened. His mouth opened as outrage crossed his expression. "You can't seriously think I had anything to do with that!"

"Where have you been the last few days?"

"In Jackson Hole. I opened a second

Watson Motors garage there. You can ask my employees," Garrett said.

"Oh, we will," Chase said. "Tell me about the posts you made on the social media pages of the Elk Valley High reunion."

Garrett's face scrunched up in confusion. "Posts? I have no idea what you're talking about."

"Really?" Chase laid the file folder on the table, opened it, and spun the file around so Garrett could read the page. "These posts, which are quite vehemently opposed to the upcoming reunion, all trace back to your ISP address."

Garrett looked at the page. A frown marred his brow. "I didn't send those. Ask Zoe." He looked up at Chase. "She knows I was totally on board with the idea of the reunion."

Yes, she had said the same. But Garrett could have just been paying her lip service. "If that's so, who made these posts and sent them from your account?"

Garrett sat back and crossed his arms over his beefy chest. "You're the experts.

Somebody must've hacked my computer or my email account. You hear about that happening all the time online."

Convenient excuse. "We need to see your computer and have access to your accounts," Chase said.

A smirk crossed his face. "Do you have a warrant?"

Garrett's smug tone grated on Chase's nerves.

"I can get a warrant," Chase told him, barely holding on to his annoyance. "That will take time." He shrugged. "But if you insist. You can wait here. It might not come through until tomorrow or the next day."

"You can't leave me in this room for days on end. That's illegal," Garrett said.

"True. But I can put you in a cell on a twenty-four-hour hold until we get that warrant."

All smugness left Garrett. He splayed his hands on the table. "You're arresting me?"

"I will if I have to," Chase told him, knowing full well he wouldn't go that far. Yet. But holding him as a person of interest wasn't out of bounds. "This would go a lot smoother if you cooperate."

For a long moment, Garrett remained silent. "Where's Zoe and Kylie?"

Chase raised an eyebrow at the change of topic. Did the man really expect anyone to believe he cared? "They're safe."

"I want to see them," Garrett said. "I want to make sure for myself."

"I think that can be arranged…if you cooperate." Chase wasn't above a trade-off. If Zoe agreed. But Chase kept that tidbit to himself.

Anger flashed in Garrett's eyes. "Fine. My computer is in my truck."

Chase glanced at Rocco and gave a nod. Rocco dipped out of the room in search of the computer.

"Were you friends with Evan Carr? Or Ryan York?"

Garrett shook his head. "No way. They were too good for the likes of me. Them and that club."

"You mean the Young Rancher's Club?" Neither Evan nor Ryan had been members, but Chase didn't feel the need to reveal that information.

"Yeah, that's the one," Garrett said. "I was the son of a mechanic. What did I know of ranching?"

"So you weren't invited to their shindigs?"

"Nope. Good thing, too, since it seems like all those golden boys have fallen victim to the Rocky Mountain Killer, eh?"

"So it seems." Chase made a mental note to go back through the Elk Valley high school yearbooks to see if there were pictures or places where Garrett intersected with Evan or Ryan or the other members of the Young Rancher's Club. Did the man have a knife tattoo on his right forearm? "Roll up your right sleeve."

"Excuse me?" Garrett scowled. "Why?"

"Is there a reason you won't?" Chase pressed.

Garrett's scowl deepened but he complied. He undid the button at his wrist and yanked the sleeve up to his elbow. No tattoo. "Satisfied?"

More like disappointed. Chase gave a nod. "Yes."

The door to the interrogation room opened and Rocco stepped back inside. "Isla's taking a look at the computer now."

Chase was a man of his word. He rose from the chair. "I'll let Zoe know you're here. If she wants to see you, then so be it. But it's her choice."

Garrett frowned. His hands clenched into fists. "I deserve to see my daughter. After all, I have to pay child support. I don't care if I see Zoe."

It took all of Chase's restraint not to launch himself across the table at Garrett and throttle the man. Instead, he gave him a clenched-jaw nod and left the room, shutting the door with a hard click behind him.

Taking several deep breaths, Chase headed for his office. His gaze went to the bed usually occupied by Dash. He missed his dog. He missed Zoe.

Giving himself a mental head slap, he picked up the phone and dialed the house number.

His father picked up on the second ring. "Rawlston's."

"Hey, Dad," Chase said. "I need to talk to Zoe."

"Here she is."

In the background, Chase could hear Liam telling Zoe that Chase was on the line.

A moment later, Zoe's sweet voice came through to tickle Chase's ear. "Hi, Chase. Is everything okay?"

"Yes. There's been a development," he said carefully. "Garrett is here and wants to see Kylie. Officer Steve can bring you over."

The silence on the other end of the line reached out and grabbed Chase by the throat. He wished he were there with her right now, letting her know it would be okay.

"We'll be right there," Zoe said, her voice devoid of any inflection.

Long after Chase hung up, he stared out the window to the park visible down the street. In the distance, the Laramie Mountains rose like sentinels watching over the valley floor.

The overwhelming need to pray rose within Chase. He tried to fight it. But the more he did, the more agitation swarmed through his system like bees after their nest was disturbed.

Staring at those mountains, he gave over to the swelling in his soul. *"Okay, Lord. I've ignored You for a long time. You have my attention. Now I want Yours. We need this to wrap up. We need to find the person who wants Zoe dead. We need to find the RMK. I need these wins."*

A check in his internal conscience made him wince. He was making it all about him. With a heavy sigh, he said, *"Forgive me, Lord. But please, help me."*

Zoe mechanically went through the process of changing Kylie's diaper and putting on a fresh cute outfit. Her mind felt numb. Garrett wanted to see Kylie. After all this time. Why? Was he going to fight her for custody? Was he going to blame the explosion on her? Her hands shook as she reached for the donated diaper bag. Liam came up to her and put a soothing hand on her shoulder. Much like she'd seen him do with his son after that awful car tried to run them down.

"Take a breath," Liam said. "Tell me what's wrong."

Zoe clamped her mouth shut. She didn't want to burden Liam with her problems. But the more she tried to hold in the torment, the more pressure built in her chest. Finally, she just gushed out all the angst gathering inside her, telling Liam about her failed marriage. About Garrett abandoning her and Kylie five days after Kylie was born. Serving her divorce papers one month later. And now he wanted to see Kylie. "I'm afraid I'll lose her."

Liam's face hardened. Anger snapped in his eyes. Eyes like his son's. "Neither Chase nor I will let that happen. I'll go with you to the station."

Dash rose from where he'd sprawled out near the front door. After a good stretch, he came and leaned against Zoe. Comfort radiated off the dog. "Are you sure he's not a therapy dog?"

"Not technically," Liam said. "But he was with Chase during the dark days. I think Dash is the only reason Chase didn't spiral farther down into the abyss after Elsa and Tommy's death."

Her heart ached at Chase's loss. "That makes sense," Zoe said running her fingers through the fur behind Dash's ears. "He's a multipurpose dog. Bomb-sniffing, protection and therapy."

Liam smiled. "Yes, to all of that."

Liam leashed up Dash while she strapped Kylie into her stroller. Liam escorted Zoe and Kylie out the door. Liam explained to Officer Steve that they were headed to the police station. The tall officer fell into step with them. Zoe felt like a celebrity with two bodyguards walking on either side of her. Only there was nothing to celebrate in this gauntlet walk to the police station to see her ex-husband.

Zoe spied Garrett's silver four-by-four

truck with the Watson Motors logo on the side door parked in the back lot at the police station. Her stomach cramped. She disliked that truck and everything it represented. When Garrett had insisted on buying the vehicle, he'd used the money they'd put aside to do renovations on the house. The house that, thankfully, Zoe had retained ownership of after the divorce proceedings. Though Garrett had tried to take it from her. He'd wanted to sell the place and split the proceeds. But the judge had sided with Zoe's lawyer, stating that Kylie needed a stable home. Besides, the house had been in Zoe's family long before she married Garrett.

More butterflies took flight in her stomach when she and Liam and Kylie entered the police station. Chase met them, giving her a sympathetic smile. She fought the urge to request a hug. Instead, she returned the smile.

"He's in the conference room," Chase said. "I thought that would be better than an interrogation room. For you and Kylie."

Her heart melted that he'd arranged for the meeting to be held in a less traumatic place, not for Garrett's sake, but for hers and her child's. She pushed the stroller and followed Chase through the police station. As they drew close to the conference room, she saw Garrett through the windowed wall. He was pacing, wearing jeans and a long-sleeve green shirt that brought out the green of his hazel eyes.

Oh, he was handsome. There was no denying it. He had a nice smile with nice teeth, thanks to orthodontia. He was tall and muscled from working on motors. But how had she ever thought him charming? Once she'd seen past the mask he wore, she'd realized he was the big bad wolf in disguise. And she had been his little red riding hood. She'd trusted him. Never again.

Chase's hand landed on the small of her back as he pushed open the door. A grab bag of emotions swirled through her. She was so grateful that Chase was by her side and she didn't have to face Garrett alone.

Chase made her feel safe and cared for. An answering affection rose within her, making her aware she was letting her guard down with Chase. She needed to bolster the walls around her heart. She didn't want to fall for another charming and handsome man. Not when the wounds from her failed marriage were still so raw.

Garrett turned as she rolled the stroller into the room. Something flashed in his eyes, there and gone. But she had seen the anger plainly enough to send a shiver of unease down her spine. Then his gaze dropped to Kylie. She watched him closely. Hoping to see some softening, some sort of paternal emotion. His face was an impassive mask.

"So that's her," Garrett said.

Zoe didn't answer, but instead released Kylie from the stroller, picking her up and putting her on her hip. Stepping around the table, she intended to ask Garrett if he wanted to hold her. He stepped back, putting his hands up as if warding off an oncoming threat. She halted.

"Oh no. I just wanted to see for myself that she was safe."

Zoe's heart folded in on itself. The man really had no emotional depth. She could feel the wounds inside scabbing over. Soon they would heal. The failure of her marriage wasn't hers, it was his.

"As you can see, we are both unharmed," she said in a steady voice.

He flicked a glance at her. His gaze went back to Kylie. "I'm not going to help you rebuild the house. You got it fair and square in the divorce."

Really? He had to bring that up? She rolled her eyes and turned her back on him, heading back to the stroller. "Why are you here?"

"Ask him," Garrett's voice was rough with suppressed rage, a tone she'd heard plenty during their time together. It usually proceeded some sort of rant. One where he found fault with everything, including her.

She'd shared with Chase how Garrett had hurt her and abandoned them. Why had he summoned Garrett? Her gaze sought Chase's. "You brought him here?"

"As I told you, we discovered he is the nasty poster on the social media sites for the reunion," Chase said, in a tone that was both neutral and professional. "He's here because we needed to question him." His gaze bore into hers. "About the explosion at your home. Now that he's brought up said home—"

"Hey, I am not saying I did it!" Garrett practically yelled.

Chase turned his gaze to Garrett. "But you did bring it up, which will give us the impetus to get a warrant to search your residence and both of your businesses for any materials used in the bombing."

"Just because I discussed something with my wife—"

Zoe whirled on him. "Ex-wife."

At the same time, Chase said "Ex-wife."

Garrett waved away their words. "Yeah, yeah, whatever. Ex-wife." He pointed a finger at Kylie. "She's still my daughter.

I'm not a monster just because I don't want to be a dad. I wouldn't do anything to hurt her."

No, not a monster. Just a jerk with narcissistic tendencies. She lifted a silent prayer to God for patience and understanding, because at the moment, she had little of either. "We're done here."

Garrett's gaze bounced away from her to something over her shoulder outside the conference room. He frowned and his face lost some color. "What's she doing here?"

Zoe turned at the same time as Chase to see Ashley with Haley Newton in tow. Haley's eyes widened when she saw the tableau inside the conference room.

"Unless you're arresting me, I'm leaving," Garrett said as he made a beeline for the door.

Chase stepped out of the way. "You may go, but stay in Elk Valley until we've executed our warrants."

"If you insist," Garrett said. "I'll be at

the original Watson Motors," referring to the local mechanic shop his father started and he'd taken over before expanding.

He stormed out of the conference room, pausing briefly to look down the hallway where Haley had just disappeared, then he did an about-face and hurried out the exit of the police station.

"What was that all about?" Chase asked.

Zoe shook her head. "I don't know."

"They both seemed unnerved to see each other," Chase observed.

"It did seem like that." Zoe's blood turned to ice. "I didn't even know they knew each other." But apparently, they did. How well?

Chase's gaze searched hers, and she hoped the awful suspicions rising to poke at her weren't visible. "Are you and Kylie okay to wait here while I talk to Haley?"

She narrowed her gaze on him. "Why did you bring her here?"

He gave her a pointed look. "That is something I cannot discuss."

She hated being left in the dark. But he'd

asked her to stay. The only way she might learn what was going on with Haley and Garrett was if she complied. "We can wait here."

EIGHT

Chase walked out of the conference room with his heart in his throat. He'd seen the suspicion in Zoe's eyes. And the hurt. That same suspicion was clambering within Chase. There was something between Haley Newton and Garrett Watson.

Just what, he didn't know, yet. A look had passed between them that led Chase to believe they weren't strangers. Friends? Lovers? Adversaries? Haley's eyes had definitely widened with recognition and a flash of panic, while Garrett had clearly been spooked to see the woman.

What a strange turn of events. They'd brought Haley in for a completely different reason—her connection to one of the RMK's first victims—and now Chase was wondering at the connection between Haley and Garrett. And did that connection have anything to do with the end of Zoe's marriage?

Inside the interrogation room, Haley sat at the table.

Ashley stood quietly near the door.

This was the third time on the same day that Chase had sat across from someone he was questioning. So why did he feel as if he wasn't making any progress?

He wasn't any closer to catching the RMK or the person who blew up Zoe's home.

Haley watched him with wary eyes. She wasn't dressed in scrubs as she had been when he'd met her at the hospital with Zoe and Kylie. Today Haley wore a gray cardigan over a white blouse and blue jeans. Her blond hair was held back by a clip. Apparently not a workday.

He decided to let the silence stretch.

She fidgeted in her seat. Finally, she asked in a voice laced with irritation, "Well? What am I doing here?"

Deciding to table Haley and Garrett's possible association and dive into the reason they'd asked her to come to the police station, Chase said, "What was your relationship to Brad Kingsley?"

Haley blanched. Her mouth dropped open. She slammed it shut. "I don't know what you mean."

From behind him, Ashley stirred. He turned to look at the rookie and motioned her forward. Chase stood and gestured for Ashley to sit. She gave him a curious look before she sat and turned her gaze on Haley. Chase hoped that because this was Ashley's intel, maybe she would make more inroads with the other woman.

"We understand that you were engaged to Brad Kingsley." Ashley's voice was friendly and gentle.

Apparent shock flashed across Haley's face then tears welled in her eyes. "Why are you asking me this? Brad died a long time ago."

"Is it true?" Ashley reached across the table to take the other woman's hand.

"Were you and Brad in love? Planning to get married?"

Haley glanced at Chase and then back at Ashley. She sniffed, then said, "Yes. We were. His snobby parents didn't approve. They wanted some Ivy League debutante. Brad and I were going to run away after graduation."

"Why didn't you tell the police about this after Brad's murder?" Ashley probed.

Haley jerked her hand away from Ashley. "Because nobody was supposed to know. I didn't want anyone gossiping about Brad. He was dead."

"You moved out of town not long after," Chase interjected.

Keeping her gaze on Ashley, Haley said, "My parents saw how distraught I was. They knew about me and Brad. I became very despondent. They were afraid I'd hurt myself. So we moved far away and I was checked into a—facility. The doctors there helped me through the grieving process. I've made a good life for myself since then. I became a nurse to help others."

"Yet, you came back to Elk Valley," Chase said. "Why?"

"Because I was once happy here," Haley told him. She looked at Ashley. "You have to understand. We were young and in love. Returning here, being in Elk Valley, helps me to feel closer to him. I miss him."

"Where were you the night the three victims were murdered?" Chase asked.

She reared back as if struck. "What? I didn't have anything to do with the murders."

"No one is saying you did. We just need to know where you were," Ashley stated in a gentle tone.

Haley heaved a sigh, clearly relieved by Ashley's words. "I was at home waiting for Brad to text me. He didn't. Then the next day…" Her shoulders slumped slightly as sadness crossed her face.

"Did you know where Brad was going that night?" Ashley asked.

"He said he had some business to take care of," Haley said. "He asked me not to go to bed. That he would come by after.

He said he'd text when he was on his way. I waited up all night."

"Haley, do you have any ideas about who killed Brad and the others?" Ashley asked.

Haley's face crumbled and she shook her head. "The Rocky Mountain Killer. I wish I knew who it was. I'd tell you. Whoever did it has to pay."

"Do you know if Brad had any sort of beef with Evan Carr? Or Ryan York?"

Haley stilled. She glanced up. "Why do you ask?"

Something in her eyes had Chase leaning forward. He didn't like her answering a question with a question. In his experience, that usually meant the person was stalling as they tried to come up with an answer, usually a lie.

"Answer the question, Haley," Chase said.

"I know there was bad blood between all of them. Some things happened. The guys laughed and joked about the pranks they pulled."

"Pranks? Like the one they pulled on Naomi Carr?"

"Yeah," Haley grimaced. "Seth, Brad and Aaron Anderson thought it would be great fun to target Naomi. I don't know why they didn't like her. But they were so mean to her at the Valentine's Day dance. They'd convinced her Trevor Gage had only asked her to the dance as a joke. They threw spitballs at her and made fun of her. She ran out in tears." Haley shuddered. "I remember thinking that I hope they never turn on me."

"Did they turn on Shelly York?" Chase asked.

Haley's gaze dropped to the table. "Poor Shelly. She didn't deserve what happened to her."

"Do you mean the breakup with Seth Jenkins?" Ashley asked.

"Yes. Seth was so nasty. He only went out with her to try to get her to sleep with him. When she wouldn't, he broke up with her in front of the guys. Said horrible things to her and about her. The guys laughed about it for weeks," Haley said softly. "I told Brad it was cruel."

"And yet you kept his secret and stayed with him," Chase commented.

Haley's gaze snapped to his. "I was young and in love. What was I supposed to do? Blab and get my boyfriend in trouble?"

"If you'd told someone about the bullying, things might have ended differently for Shelly." Chase couldn't keep the anger from his tone. And Ryan York wouldn't be one of their prime suspects. The more Chase learned about Ryan and his beef with Seth and his friends, the more guilty Ryan appeared.

"Maybe." Haley spread her hands. "There's nothing I can do about the past now. I can only move forward. And try to be the best version of myself I can be. That's why I went into healthcare. To give back. Pay some kind of penitence for not protecting Naomi or Shelly."

"Those weren't the only pranks, though, were they?" Chase persisted. No way would they have not been up to more she-nanigans. "What other things did the guys do that were funny to them?"

Haley shrugged. "There was something to do with the caves in the mountains."

This was interesting. And the first time anyone had mentioned caves. There were multiple caves and caverns in the mountains of Wyoming to explore. Most were open to the public. Some were not. "Which caves and which mountains are we talking about?"

"The guys never said," Haley replied. "I assume the Laramie Mountains. They are the closest."

Frustrated with the lack of information, he pressed. "Who was involved? What happened during these cave incidents?"

"I don't know," she said. "I don't know anything that's going to help you. Can I go now?"

He wasn't sure she was telling him everything, but he decided it was time to change directions. "What's your relationship to Garrett Watson?"

"Garrett?" Haley's eyes darted between Chase and Ashley. "You can't suspect him? I mean, no way is he the Rocky Mountain Killer."

He supposed it made sense she'd jump straight to the RMK considering the topic of their earlier conversation. But the way she protested on Garrett's behalf was odd. "Just answer the question," Chase insisted.

"He worked on my car," she said. "Is that a crime?"

There was a hint of belligerence in her tone. "You seemed pretty shaken when you saw him in the conference room today."

"Did I?" Haley shook her head. "I didn't even realize he was in the room. I saw Zoe and her baby."

Chase wasn't buying it. He remembered how at the hospital, Haley had asked Zoe if she'd informed Garrett of the bombing. Was that how Garrett had learned of the explosion that had destroyed his ex-wife's home? Playing a hunch, Chase said, "Garrett had a bit more to say about your relationship."

Panic entered Haley's eyes. Then she blinked several times, seeming to settle herself. "Whatever. So we had a fling when I first moved to town. I didn't know then that he was married to Zoe. I broke it off as soon as I found out. If he says anything different, he's lying."

Though she confirmed what Chase suspected, it didn't make hearing of the affair any easier. His heart ached for Zoe. "We may have more questions for you down the road. But for now, don't leave Elk Valley."

"I'm free to go?" Surprise laced her tone.

"You are," Chase said as he moved to the door. "Ashley will see you home."

Chase didn't relish telling Zoe that her ex-husband had had an affair with her colleague at the hospital. But he knew he couldn't keep this from her. Eventually, it would come to light, and she would only be hurt and angry at him if she learned he'd kept the information from her. He hoped he could comfort her without it affecting him. Against his better judgment, he was already finding himself caring deeply for the mother and child.

Zoe pushed the stroller for the umpteenth time in a lap around the conference table. At least she was getting in some steps. Kylie finally conked out and slept. A glance at the clock confirmed Chase had been gone for over an hour interviewing Haley in an interrogation room. What were they discussing? What was Haley and Garrett's connection?

She tried to think back over the past to see if she remembered Garrett or Haley ever meeting. But nothing came to mind. Garrett had never mentioned Haley, and other than recently at the hospital when Haley asked if Garrett had been informed about the explosion, Haley had never mentioned Garrett. Yet they both had reacted peculiarly when they'd seen each other.

Zoe paused mid-lap to grab the water bottle Liam had brought her and took a long swig.

The door to the conference room opened and Chase stepped inside.

Glad to see him and anxious for answers, Zoe pushed the stroller with a sleeping Kylie to meet him at the head of the table.

"What can you tell me?" she asked softly, knowing he wouldn't divulge anything regarding the Rocky Mountain Killer investigation.

But he would divulge information regarding the explosion at her home, wouldn't he?

Chase gestured to a chair. "Please, have a seat."

Trepidation spread through Zoe as she maneuvered the stroller around so that she could sit and keep an eye on Kylie at the same time.

Once they were seated, their chairs facing each other and their knees nearly touching, Chase said quietly, "What I have to tell you is going to be hard to hear."

Her stomach dropped. That suspicion she'd had earlier raised to the forefront of her mind. "Are Haley and Garrett involved?"

He grimaced. Clearly uncomfortable. "Apparently, Haley didn't realize Garrett was married when she first arrived back in town," Chase said carefully. "Once she realized he was your husband she broke off the relationship."

Zoe couldn't assess how she felt about this revelation. Her husband had had an affair. She calculated back to when Haley had first come on board as a nurse at the Elk Valley Community Hospital. Three years ago. Around the time Garrett had taken over Watson Motors from his father, who'd retired and moved to Arizona.

Garrett had poured himself and their savings into the business. Bringing the auto-body shop into the twenty-first century, he'd claimed. At the time, Zoe had tried to be supportive even if she'd been lonely because Garrett spent so little time at home. Now she understood why.

Zoe should be shocked. But all she felt was numb. Her husband had had an affair. Long before he abandoned her and their child. She couldn't even claim his desertion on another woman.

Chase gathered her hands in his. His were warm and comforting against the flood of ice in her veins. She curled her fingers over his. Wanting, no needing, his strength and steady presence, even though relying on him wasn't a smart move. "I'd been so gullible. I mean, I suspected at times that he might be…" She swallowed back the recriminations that laid shame and blame on her doorstep. She would not own his bad behavior. His betrayal. "He told me I was being paranoid."

"Are you okay?"

Chase's soft voice grabbed her focus. The concern and compassion on his face made her want to fling herself into his arms. She squeezed his fingers. "I will be. It's a lot to process."

She needed time on her own to sort through the quagmire of her emotions. She couldn't do that with Chase so close and the temptation to lean on him for comfort and support so strong. She tugged her hands from his and stood. She had to get out of there. She needed to go someplace where she could think and pray and rage.

Chase rose to his full height, eating up the distance between them.

There was nowhere for her to go. Literally and figuratively. Her home had been blown up. Her parents lived far away. She was trapped by her isolation. And by the chair behind her, the stroller on one side and the table on the other.

And Chase stood in front of her. A handsome warrior, yet a gentle man.

Her heart battered against her rib cage. A yearning swelled within her. She met his gaze and saw the same yearning in his eyes.

His hand came up to cup her cheek, and she didn't flinch or shy away, despite her earlier need to escape. Her feet felt glued to the floor and her heart calmed. His touch was tender and light against her skin, melting the ice in her veins.

"You deserve so much better," he said, in a near whisper.

Was he talking about Garrett? Or himself?

Either way, she would decide what she deserved. Never again would she let someone else dictate her life.

And at this moment, she wanted, needed, the affirmation that she would be okay. That she was a beautiful woman who could attract a man like Chase.

She swayed toward him, the distance between them reduced to a millimeter. Questions and curiosity shone brightly in his eyes for a moment before he dipped his head and captured her lips.

The kiss was soft, probing and so welcome.

She entwined her arms around his neck, going up on tiptoe to better match him. All the hurt crowding her chest was pushed aside by a flood of warmth and affection for this man.

The soft snick of the door opening and the clearing of a throat jerked them apart.

Zoe stumbled, nearly falling back into the chair but managing to push it out of the way with the back of her knees. She skirted around the edge of the stroller and gripped the handle before she lifted her gaze to the person standing at the conference room entrance.

A woman she'd never seen before smiled hesitantly. A blonde with bright blue eyes. She wore a jacket with the MCK9 logo on the front.

Desperate to escape as embarrassment flushed through her system, Zoe asked Chase, "Your father? Where is he?"

"The break room," Chase said, his voice husky. "Down the hall to your right. You can't miss it."

Without looking at him, she gave a quick nod then pushed the stroller past the woman standing in the doorway and headed in the direction Chase had mentioned. Her cheeks flamed. What was she doing? How could she let that kiss happen?

Oh no, her conscience chided. *You made this happen.*

And as much as she should regret kissing Chase, and probably would tomorrow, right now, she didn't regret it. At all.

Chase stood frozen in place. His whole body felt on fire. He slowly turned to see who had interrupted the moment of insanity.

CSI Ophelia Clarke.

The embarrassment crowding his chest reflected in her pretty face. Man, was he losing it to kiss Zoe in the police station. Had the parallels to his wife's death made him more invested in this case than he should have been? And now that he'd come to know and care for Zoe, he was getting in too deep. Allowing such unprofessional behavior wasn't like him. He needed to do better at keeping his emotions in check.

"Sorry," Ophelia said. "I didn't realize until I'd already—"

He held up a hand. "Not your fault. Just keep this between us, shall we?"

"Mum's the word," Ophelia said, coming all the way into the room. "I thought you'd want to know right away that the remnants of the bomb used to blow up Zoe Jenkins's home was homemade. Rudimentary."

He blew out an aggravated breath. "So basically, anyone with the understanding of engineering…?"

Ophelia made a face. "Anyone with access to the internet can watch videos of how to build an explosive device like the one used," she said.

Acid bore a hole through his gut. "We're back to square one. We still don't know who could have planted the bomb."

Ophelia raised a piece of paper he hadn't noticed she held. "I made a list of the ingredients and supplies needed. They can be purchased at any hardware-type store."

"Give that to Ian and Meadow," he said. "They can check with the local stores. Can you and Kyle make a wider search?"

"Of course, we can."

"Thank you," Chase said. "I need to call the team together and let them know what I've learned from Haley Newton."

Ophelia stuck a hand in the pocket of her

jacket and pulled out her cell phone. "I can text everyone if you'd like."

Running a hand down his face in an attempt to steady his breathing, Chase said, "I'd appreciate it. Also, can you check on the BOLO on Dr. Webb's stolen car? If they find it, I want you to process it for any evidence."

"Glad to do it," she said.

Meeting her gaze, Chase swallowed at the understanding and speculation in her eyes. Keeping his expression carefully neutral, he strode out of the conference room confident Ophelia would assemble the team while he went in search of Zoe and Kylie. His chest warmed at the thought of Zoe. *Stop*. He was protecting a vulnerable woman and child. Nothing more.

Then why did you kiss her?

He had no explanation and didn't want to examine his actions too closely.

The break room where he'd expected to find his father, Kylie, Dash and Zoe was empty.

He hustled out the exit in time to see Zoe

flanked by his dad, who held Dash's leash, and Officer Steve, quickly making their way down the sidewalk. Confident that the men and his dog would keep Zoe and Kylie safe, Chase went to the men's room and splashed water on his face. "Brilliant move, Rawlston," he said to his reflection.

He'd have to do damage control with Zoe when he got home tonight. He didn't want her to be hurt or to be thinking there was something more to their relationship than there was. More than he could allow.

But right now, he had a plan to set in motion.

NINE

Within the hour, the team had gathered in the conference room. Rocco stood near the window overlooking the parking lot, his chocolate lab, Cocoa, beside him. Seated around the long oval table were Meadow, Ian, Ashley and Bennett. Their respective dogs either sat beside their handler's chair or lay down at their feet beneath the table.

Chase had requested a whiteboard be brought in and placed where all could see it.

Along the top, he made two columns with the headings RMK and Unsub, referring to the unidentified subject targeting Zoe.

The large monitor screen facing the conference table was split with Trevor and Hannah videoing in from the safe house in Utah. On the other side of the screen was Selena and her private investigator fiancé, Finn Donovan.

The most recent text Chase had received from the RMK had put searches in other Rocky Mountain states on hold. Presumably, the RMK lurked somewhere in Elk Valley now. A horrible problem they needed to deal with.

"Let's go over what we know so far." Chase wrote on the whiteboard in red marker. "If the text is to be believed, our serial killer is in town for the reunion."

"Do you still think the RMK plans on trying to kill Trevor at the reunion?" Ashley asked.

"He can't," Hannah said. "We aren't coming."

"Well, that's the thing," Chase said. "We need the RMK to believe Trevor is going to be at the reunion."

"You hope he shows up?" Trevor said. "As I said before, I can't remember if I RSVP'd, but I could post on the reunion social media pages saying I'm heading back to town."

"Good idea." Chase wrote that down on the blackboard. "I will also ask Zoe to spread the news that you're coming."

Hannah scowled. "When do you want us there?"

"I don't," Chase said.

"You just want RMK to think I'm coming," Trevor said. "To what end?"

There was a murmur of agreement to the question that rippled through the room.

"I have a plan, which I will tell you about in a moment." He wrote on the whiteboard. *Kidnapped Cowgirl but released puppies.* "We at least know he's got a heart when it comes to animals."

"Small comfort to those he's killed," Bennett said.

"Agreed. We have two suspects." He wrote the names *Evan Carr* and *Ryan York* on the board. He filled the task force in on what Haley had said about Naomi Carr and Shelly York.

"The victims—and Trevor—were all

part of the same group of friends," Chase said. "With the exception of Peter and Trevor, they played cruel pranks on those they didn't like. And the RMK targeted them. Peter was killed for being a part of the pack. The RMK went after Trevor but wasn't successful."

Trevor scrubbed a hand over his jaw. "I just want this over."

"We all do," Chase said. Then he told them about Zoe's ex-husband. "For half a second I thought maybe Garrett Watson might be added to the list of RMK suspects, but he doesn't have a knife tattoo on his right forearm."

Chase moved to the column he'd drawn under the bomber of Zoe's house. He wrote *RMK* with a question mark beside it. "I haven't ruled out that the Rocky Mountain Killer isn't after Zoe, though there haven't been any attacks on the other family members of the victims. It seems less likely." He shrugged. "The ex-husband? Garrett Watson showed little regard for Zoe's welfare, but he did come to town to make sure his daughter, whom he claims not to want, was safe."

"There's still the question of the people who are against having the reunion and what lengths they might go to stop it," Ashley said.

"We worked our way through all of the names on the list Zoe gave us and those who made the negative comments on social media," Meadow said. "Other than Garrett Watson, no one else stands out as a possible suspect."

"I concur, boss," Rocco said. "There were many names that were from an older generation who are either infirm or have limited mobility. All the others have alibis for the days leading up to the explosion. Nothing came from the canvass of Zoe's neighborhood either. Whoever planted the bomb did so under the cover of night and was careful not to be seen by any exterior cameras."

"Which might suggest the person responsible has to be someone who is familiar with the neighborhood." Unease slithered down Chase's spine. Could one of Zoe's neighbors have a reason to target her? "What do we know about those living in close proximity to Zoe?"

"Most weren't home at the time of the explosion," Meadow said. "But we can do background checks on them all. Did Zoe mention if there was any sort of conflict with her neighbors?"

Chase shook his head. "I'll ask her about that when I get home."

He didn't miss the exchange of speculative glances among the team. He should disabuse them of the idea there was anything untoward going on between him and Zoe, but for some reason he held his tongue. Ophelia had seen them kiss and had promised to keep it to herself. Were his growing feelings for Zoe beginning to show? He needed to do a better job of keeping his emotions under wraps.

The door to the conference room opened and Kyle and his K-9 partner, Rocky, a male coonhound with long floppy ears, stepped inside, drawing not only the humans' attention but also that of the dogs in the room.

"Hey, wanted to let you know that Dr. Webb's car was found in the parking lot of the hospital," Kyle said. "Ophelia's processing it as we speak." He and Rocky moved farther inside so he could shut the door. "And I just had a very interesting conversation with the clerk who likely sold our suspected bomber the supplies."

Chase's pulse jumped. "Please, tell me you have a description or better yet, a photo."

Kyle shook his head. "Sorry. The clerk said the person paid with cash and only gave grunted responses. The clerk couldn't say whether the suspect was a man or a woman. The store's security video feed, which I finally managed to get from the owner of the shop, shows a slim figure wearing dark clothes, a hoodie pulled up over a baseball cap, and oversized dark glasses covering most of their face. The purchase was made two weeks before the bombing."

Not a spur of the moment decision. "The suspect is a planner." The thought sent dread coursing through his veins. What was the person targeting Zoe planning next?

"Thank you, Kyle, for your hard work," Chase said. "And please have Ophelia contact me the moment she's done."

Teeming with frustration, Chase shoved a hand through his hair. They were still no closer to knowing who destroyed Zoe's home, but he hoped the car would reveal something about the person who'd tried to run them down. Were the bomber and the car thief the same person?

He put down the whiteboard marker, ready to lay out his plan. "Here's my idea. Feel free to poke holes in it. I want to get this right. Trevor is the only surviving target from that old friend group. Starting tomorrow, we are going to spread the rumor that Trevor is coming to town for the reunion. I'm going to rent a house on the outskirts of town in Trevor's name. On the night of the reunion, a small team will lie in wait for the RMK to make his move."

"What if he tries to make his move at the reunion?" Trevor asked, his voice tinny over the video feed. "You need me there."

"I have a workaround for that," Chase said. "At the reunion, we'll tell people you're in town staying at a rental but not feeling well. But before the reunion, I'll drive around town pretending to be you. We're roughly the same height and build. I'll need one of your signature silver Stetsons and access to a truck with your company logo on it."

"Thus, forcing the RMK to go to the house in order to attack Trevor," Rocco said.

"Exactly." Chase could see that the team was on board with the plan.

"Or the RMK could try to off you as Trevor as you're driving around," Bennett pointed out.

"True," Chase said. "Which is why one of you will follow at a discreet distance. And we can communicate via earwigs," he explained, referring to the communication devices that allowed them to hear each other through a small earplug.

"I can do that," Bennett said.

"Great. One other issue... I need someone to provide protection for Zoe at the reunion in case we haven't found the person targeting her by then." Chase didn't want to have to pick someone but rather hoped for a volunteer.

There was definitely an uncomfortable silence echoing through the room as the ramifications of what Chase was asking became clear. If they didn't discover who was targeting Zoe and Kylie soon, one of the task force members would be on protection detail and not in on the serial killer's potential arrest.

"I'll do it," Meadow and Ashley said at the same time.

Gratitude for the two team members and their willingness filled Chase. "Thank you both. Meadow, you stay with Zoe. Be her shadow at the reunion." At her nod, he said, "I appreciate it. Ashley, would Cade be willing to go with you to the reunion?"

"We were already planning on going," Ashley said. "My sister-in-law Melissa and her bestie, Jessie, are both planning on attending, as well."

"Good. If you all could keep your eyes and ears open, and spread the word that Trevor's in town but not feeling well, that would be optimal." Chase turned his focus to Rocco. "The same for you. You're alumni and your presence there won't be questioned, plus Sadie's on the reunion committee so it makes sense for you to be there."

"But you're also alumni," Bennett pointed out.

"True," Chase said. "I'll make an appearance early on and then duck out."

"While you're doing that," Ian said, "I'll be waiting in the house."

"Good. I'll show up driving Trevor's truck, in case the RMK is watching."

"I can stay and help with the takedown,"

Kyle said. He looked to Ian. "I'll join you at the house."

Ian nodded. "Sounds good."

"I'd appreciate that," Chase said. "We'll also have Deputy US Marshal Sully Briggs on standby. He'll take the RMK into custody and get him far from town as quickly as possible."

"That's a good idea," Rocco said. "There's a long line of people who would like a chance to rip into the Rocky Mountain Killer."

"Exactly," Chase said. "We want the RMK to stand trial and answer for his crimes. Not be killed in some vigilante assassination."

"I can take care of renting the house," Bennett said.

"I can make the trip to Utah and drive one of Trevor's company trucks back here," Ian said.

Pride and pleasure swelled within Chase's chest. He couldn't have asked for a better task force than the men and women sitting around the table and on the screen.

Each member of the team had a specialty K-9 dog, and the combination made them a fierce force to be reckoned with.

"You guys are the best," Chase said. "I'll have Isla make the posts on Trevor's behalf routing the ISP through his company."

Chase released the team to go about their assignments. They had three days to prepare for the takedown of the Rocky Mountain Killer.

Failure wasn't an option. Not again. This time the task force would succeed. Chase sent up a silent prayer asking God for help. And doing so eased some of the anxiousness bouncing around his chest.

After putting Kylie in the playpen that now took up space in the living room, Zoe set the table while Chase cooked in the kitchen. He'd shooed her out moments ago, telling her he had everything under his control. It wasn't often somebody, offered to cook for Zoe, outside of when she went to a restaurant. Usually, once people knew that she was a chef and a dietitian, they asked her to do the cooking.

But Chase and his father, Liam, both seemed to enjoy the culinary arts. She would appreciate whatever they put in front of her.

Dash scrambled from his place near the front door as Liam appeared in the dining room doorway. He was dressed up in chino slacks and a gray blazer over a blue button-down shirt. His hair was combed and styled. And he'd recently shaved. "You don't have to set a place for me."

Chase came out behind him and Zoe's breath caught. The man was too handsome for his own good. He still had on his work uniform but now a white apron covered the front of him, and the words *Kiss the Cook* stenciled in blue seemed to shout at Zoe, reminding her of the kiss in the conference room. Heat infused her cheeks, and she hoped the men didn't notice. She and Chase needed to talk about the kiss. About what the kiss meant. Or didn't mean.

She usually didn't shy away from hard

conversations but for some reason, this one had her pulse skittering every time she thought about broaching the subject.

Chase folded his arms over his chest. "Dad, where're you going?"

"Out," Liam said, obvious excitement evident on his face.

"Okay," Chase said slowly. "Where? And what time will you be home?"

A scowl darkened Liam's face. "I don't think that's any of your business."

"I think it's lovely that you're going out. Hopefully to do something fun?" Zoe ventured, slanting a glance at Chase to gauge his reaction.

He turned his thunderous gaze to her. She lifted her chin.

"Zoe, if you don't mind—"

"I appreciate your support, Zoe," Liam broke in before Chase could finish his words.

Chase grimaced, running a hand down his face. "I just want to make sure everyone stays safe. With the RMK in town, we have no idea who will be his next target. The police department has extra patrols canvassing all areas of town and the FBI and US Marshals are here as backup and also stationed around town, keeping an eye out."

Zoe's heart melted a little, and she reached out a hand to place it on Chase's forearm. "We all appreciate your protectiveness. I'm sure your father will be careful. And it sounds like you and your team have covered all the bases. There's only so much you can control."

Liam's expression softened. "Yes, we all do appreciate your efforts. I'm going to the Rusty Spoke. It's trivia night. I'll be fine, surrounded by lots of people."

Chase's jaw set in a hard line. Zoe waited to see if he would demand an escort go with his father. But instead, he heaved a sigh. "I hope you have a good time."

Remembering the flirtatious vibe she'd witnessed between Liam and Martha Baldwin, she asked, "Will Martha Baldwin be there?"

Liam grinned. "She will. Don't wait up."

After Liam left, Chase turned to stare at Zoe. "You must think I am…" He spread his hands wide. "I'm not even sure what to say. He's my dad and I can't stand the thought of something happening to him."

"And I'm sure he has the same thoughts every time you walk out the door," Zoe said gently.

Chase seemed to think that over then gave a nod. "You're right, of course. I'm on edge. No closer to catching your bomber. I see threats everywhere."

"It's understandable," she said. "But you can't let fear rule you."

"Sometimes it's hard not to," he said, his voice breaking.

She understood. After what happened to his wife and son, Chase had become hypervigilant, wanting to keep those he loved safe. In some small measure, she and Kylie were both in that circle now. Though she couldn't say he loved her, he did care. She couldn't deny that, just as she couldn't deny she cared for him. More than cared, if she were being honest, but her developing feelings would only lead to disappoint-ment. Heartache. The attraction between her and Chase was born out of a stressful and dangerous situation. It couldn't last, could it?

"When I'm afraid, I will trust in the Lord," she said. "That's my mantra most days. It's been hard and daunting to think about raising Kylie alone. But I know that God has me in His hands. I know He has you and Liam and the task force and this town in His hands. Circumstances may not turn out the way we want. In fact, they rarely do. That doesn't negate God's good-ness."

Chase covered her hand on his arm with his own and threaded their fingers together. He brought her hand to his lips and kissed her knuckles. "You are a brave and wise woman. Zoe, I—"

The sound of the buzzer cut off his words. "The lasagna is done." He let go of her hand and returned to the kitchen, leav-ing Zoe to wonder what he had been about to say. Was he going to bring up their kiss?

Her pulse sped up as she transferred Kylie from the playpen to the high chair set up at the dining table. She had to work to calm her breathing as Chase brought out the pan of lasagna and a bowl of fresh green salad. He also placed a plastic bowl filled with small chunks of fruit in front of Kylie. Tenderness flooded Zoe at his thoughtfulness toward her daughter.

Chase dished up the lasagna and Zoe scooped salad onto their plates. They ate and chatted about life, books and art in a companionable way that put her at ease. Chase asked about her business and seemed genuinely interested in hearing her ideas for how to expand once her house was restored.

A pang hit her square in the chest.

How often had she longed for someone to share meals with? Someone to share her hopes and dreams with? Garrett had hardly ever been home for dinner and hadn't really been easy to confide in. The man was adept at turning the conversation to him whenever she'd tried to open up.

"I have a favor to ask of you," Chase said as he pushed his empty plate away.

Grateful to help him in whatever way, she said, "Okay."

He laughed. "You haven't even heard what it is."

She shrugged. "I owe you my life and Kylie's life. Whatever you need."

He tilted his head. "You don't owe me anything. I was doing my job."

Gesturing to the table and the house, she said, "And all of this, is just you doing your job?"

His lips curved in a half smile that was both endearing and amusing. "Maybe."

Her heart did a little jig. "What are we doing?"

His eyes widened. "What do you mean?"

"Don't play coy," she said. "We both feel the attraction."

"Attraction, yes," Chase said. "How could I not? You're a beautiful, funny, smart and caring person. But I'm not in a position to offer you anything."

Just a kiss. Her heart hurt. But what

did she expect? "I understand," she said. "You're still grieving the loss of your wife and child. And, frankly, I don't know if I could ever truly trust my heart to a man again."

"Don't say that." Chase reached out to take her hand. "Don't paint every man with the same brush as your ex-husband. There are good men out there. You'll find the right one someday."

"Right." But it was clear he didn't consider himself the right one. She should be relieved, but instead a bruise lashed across her heart. She extracted her hand. "What was that favor?"

He hesitated then said, "I need you to help me spread the word that Trevor Gage is returning for the reunion."

"Does this have something to do with the Rocky Mountain Killer?"

He pressed his lips together. Obviously, he couldn't say.

"Never mind," she said and stood. "We can start now. Let me change Kylie into a warm outfit and we can head downtown for ice cream."

"Ice cream in October?"

"Yep. Pumpkin spice ice cream," she said, though she really didn't have much of an appetite now. "Plus, if we mention Trevor coming home to Simon Kimmer, the owner of the shop, he'll spread the word."

"Thank you," Chase said.

Zoe released Kylie from her high chair and headed for the bedroom. She could feel Chase's gaze, so she kept her head high and her shoulders back. No way would she let him know how his words had affected her. And reinforced her need to not rely on anyone else.

Chase watched Zoe walk into the spare bedroom and shut the door. The air in the house seemed to cool, or maybe it was just his blood. He'd hurt her. Unintentionally but still…his shoulders dropped with the weight of regret.

"Son?"

Chase whirled around to find his father standing in the shadows of the entryway. "How long have you been there?"

"Long enough," Liam stepped to the entryway cabinet, opened a drawer, and removed his wallet. "I forgot this and came back for it. I didn't mean to overhear."

Chase ran his hand through his hair. "What do I do? How do I make this right with Zoe?"

"You care for her," Liam said.

"Yes. But it can't go anywhere. My heart is too broken."

"Hearts mend when you let them. You are not responsible for Elsie's or Tommy's deaths."

This was an old argument between them. Chase remained silent, not seeing the point of debating his guilt when nothing could assuage it.

"I miss Elsie and Tommy," Liam continued. "I miss your mother something fierce." He moved to stand in front of his son. "But it's time to let go of the past. Forgive yourself. Elsie wouldn't want you to be alone. And I know your mother wouldn't have wanted me to be alone. I've been alone too long."

Chase wasn't sure how to respond or even how to sort through the emotions swirling through him. Forgive himself? How? "But in moving on, won't I forget them?"

"Never. They will always have a place in our hearts. But it's time to put the past behind us. And look to the future."

"It's hard for me to think beyond the next few days," Chase replied out of self-preservation. His focus had to be on putting an end to the RMK's reign of terror. And he still had to find the person targeting Zoe. Until then he had to control his emotions and stay professional.

"You'll know when the time is right," Liam told him as he opened the door to leave. "The time is right for me. I'm going to ask Martha Baldwin out on a date."

For a long moment after his father left, Chase stared at the closed door. He was happy for his dad; he was brave to put his heart out there again. And he was right, his mom wouldn't have wanted or expected his dad to be alone forever. Just as Elsie wouldn't have wanted or expected Chase to be alone. But could Chase be as brave as his father when he still had so much guilt and sorrow pressing down on him?

TEN

Zoe forced a smile as she pushed Kylie in the stroller down the sidewalk of Main Street. The evening breeze swept over her face, cooling her cheeks. Chase, with Dash on a leash, walked beside her while behind them, Officer Steve strolled along keeping a discreet distance but close enough to be of use if anything should happen.

Trying not to view every person they passed with suspicion, she waved at several of the townsfolk who she was acquainted with. When they reached the ice cream parlor, she heard the faint ding of the bell over the door as Mayor Singh and his wife and two young children filed out.

"Zoe Jenkins," the mayor boomed. "So good to see you." He shifted his gaze to

Chase. "Agent Rawlston. I hope you're taking good care of Zoe and will put whoever destroyed her home behind bars soon."

"That is the plan, Mayor," Chase answered.

"Again, I'm so sorry about the meals—" Zoe started to say but was cut off when the mayor held up a hand. He'd been so gracious when she'd called to tell him the meals she'd prepared for him had been destroyed.

"Nonsense," the mayor said. "Not your fault."

"We'll get him on that paleo diet eventually," his wife said with a smile. "It's more important that you stay safe."

"Thank you both," Zoe said.

The mayor and his family waved and headed down the street.

Chase opened the door to the ice cream parlor and looked in. "It's pretty crowded in here. Should we leave the stroller outside?"

Always thoughtful, this one. "Yes." She quickly unbuckled the straps and picked

Kylie up, placing her on her hip. "What about Dash?"

"He can fit," Chase said and gestured for her to enter.

Zoe carried Kylie into the ice cream parlor. The smells of sugar and waffle cones brought back memories of summers as a kid riding her bike to the ice cream parlor with her friends. The red-and-white décor harkened back to days long gone, but the nostalgia for simpler times remained.

Zoe and Chase, with Dash close at his side, stepped into line and waited their turn at the counter behind several people ordering.

"Good evening," the young adult woman with a name tag that read Cindy said as they moved to the front of the line. The ice cream case was filled with a plethora of flavors from the standard strawberry, vanilla and chocolate to seasonal flavors and creative blends.

Cindy eyed Dash, then asked, "What can I get for you tonight?"

The owner of the ice cream shop came out from the back.

"Zoe!" Mr. Kimmer, a man in his late sixties with salted dark hair and a slow gait, moved to stand beside his employee. "I've got this."

Cindy shrugged and moved away to take someone else's order.

"Are you doing okay?" Mr. Kimmer asked. "It's just awful what happened to your house. It's just awful what keeps happening in our town."

"Yes, sir, we're fine," Zoe told him, choosing to not address the last part of his statement. She didn't want to give anyone more reason to oppose the reunion. "But we have a hankering for some pumpkin spice ice cream."

Mr. Kimmer's face lit up. "I have a special pumpkin spice sundae with caramel and pecans. Would you like to try it?"

Her mouth watered at the mention of pecans. "Of course." She turned to Chase. "What about you?"

"How can I pass up a pumpkin spice sundae?" His smile was amused and tender and intimate.

Her heart thumped against her ribs. She turned away, not wanting to fall any deeper into this man's orbit. He may be attracted to her. And he cared, she didn't doubt that. But he was doing his job. She didn't know if she could be friends with him without wanting more. She hoped so because she really liked him. Though she feared there would be a cost to her heart.

"Two pumpkin spice sundaes coming up," Mr. Kimmer said. "And a pup cup for the dog?"

"Sure," Chase said. "Dash would like that."

Remembering their purpose for the outing beyond the sweet treat, Zoe said, "I hope we'll see you at the reunion."

"I'll be there," Mr. Kimmer said without enthusiasm. "I'm just not sure how wise this endeavor is at this particular time."

"Not you, too?" Zoe said. All the divisiveness the event was causing dampened her spirits a bit. Her hopes that it would bring some comfort were slipping away. "I was hoping people would see this as a good thing for the town. People from out of state who moved away long ago are coming back. Trevor Gage, in fact, is on his way here."

"Seriously?" Mr. Kimmer said. "I never thought we'd see him back in town. You know, after all that nastiness with the Rocky Mountain Killer and the Young Rancher's Club. Trevor was a part of that group of friends, wasn't he?"

"It's true Trevor had been friends with the victims," Chase said in a stern tone. "I don't think it's a good idea—or safe—for him to attend the reunion, but apparently he'll bc there."

Zoe glanced around aware that the volume of conversation in the ice cream parlor had subsided to a few whispers as everyone seemed to be listening to the conversation. She and Chase couldn't have asked for a better way to get the news out that Trevor was coming back to town.

Was one of the people sitting at the

counter or in one of the booths the Rocky Mountain Killer? A shudder of dread and apprehension worked its way through her system. Or was one of these people the person who was trying to kill her? Were they one and the same?

She was confident that whoever was targeting her wouldn't try something with Chase and Dash standing guard and Officer Steve right outside the ice cream parlor door.

"There's an open booth in the corner," Mr. Kimmer said with a wave. "I'll bring the sundaes to you."

Zoe put Kylie in a high chair, situated next to the edge of the table, then she and Chase settled in the large booth with Dash sitting at their feet underneath.

The bell over the door dinged. Zoe smiled to see her friend Sadie and her three-year-son, Myles. Myles had diabetes and had a therapy dog, an Irish setter, with him. Sadie's fiancé Rocco and his K-9, a black Lab, also stepped inside. Chase saw them as well and waved them over.

"Join us. We have room," Chase said as he stood.

Zoe wondered if he'd invited them to their table because he didn't want to be alone with her. A sadness stung her, but she shrugged it off.

Sadie scooted into the booth, settling Myles on her lap. The dogs settled under the table at their feet. Zoe marveled that the dogs all got along and were so well behaved. Nothing like the dog her parents had when she was a kid. Snickers, a Pomeranian, had been a terror, always stealing Zoe's socks and hiding them.

"I'll go place our order," Rocco said and he hustled to stand in line. His K-9 readjusted himself beneath the table so he could keep an eye on his handler.

"Isn't that Dr. Webb and his family?" Sadie gestured to the newcomers to the packed ice cream parlor. "He's been so good with Myles."

Zoe exchanged a glance with Chase. Chase had said someone had stolen the doctor's car and used the vehicle to try to run them over. By the glare on Chase's face, she surmised he wasn't happy to see the doctor. "Yes, that is Dr. Webb and his wife and son."

As if the doctor had sensed Zoe mentioning his name, he turned and waved at them. He left his family and came over to the table. "Hello, Zoe. Agent Rawlston. Sadie."

"Hi, Dr. Webb," Zoe greeted him.

Chase didn't respond, only kept his eyes trained on the doctor.

"How's Kylie?" Dr. Webb asked, his gaze on her daughter.

"She's good, no worse for the trauma," Zoe replied, aware that Chase's stare was less than welcoming. Did he still suspect Dr. Webb was behind the attacks on her and Kylie?

"Good, good. Glad to hear that," Dr. Webb said, backing up, clearly uncomfortable, before he turned and walked back to join his family.

The bell over the door jingled as more and more people entered.

Zoe settled into a conversation with Sadie about the decorations for the reunion. Though she kept an eye on Chase, who kept an eye on everyone else in the parlor.

Finally, Rocco rejoined them. "Mr. Kimmer said he'd bring our sundaes over when he brings yours." He slipped into the booth next to Sadie.

"Who knew ice cream was such a popular dessert on a late October night," Sadie said. "Maybe I need to add some ice cream to Sadie's Subs."

"It certainly couldn't hurt," Rocco said. "Everybody loves ice cream."

Zoe saw Chase nudge Rocco, then gesture with his chin toward a new group of thirtysomethings who entered the ice cream shop. "Tall, blond man."

Rocco nodded and slipped out of the booth. Chase followed him.

"We'll be right back," Chase said, his gaze on Zoe. "Don't go anywhere."

She arched an eyebrow. "Where am I going to go?"

He gave a sheepish grin and nodded.

The two men wound their way through the group, cornering the blond man.

"He's very protective of you," Sadie said with a smile lacing her words.

"It's his job. Nothing more, as he's made very clear to me."

"Yeah, Rocco tried something similar. *I don't have time for romantic entanglements*." Sadie lowered her voice to mimic the man she loved.

Zoe laughed, even as her heart gave a little bump of hope. But she quickly slammed the hope down. Not going to happen. Chase wasn't ready to move on from his late wife. And she shouldn't be ready to trust Chase with her heart, however much her traitorous heart disagreed.

Her gaze snagged on another woman who'd entered the shop and was working her way to the counter.

Haley Newton.

Bitter resentment rose within Zoe and she clenched her teeth against the tide. Turning away, she resumed the conversation about the reunion with Sadie. "We should incorporate pages from the yearbooks throughout the decades. We could frame them and set up displays around the room."

"That's a brilliant idea," Sadie said. "I was also thinking we could ask several of the high school teachers who are coming to say a few words about each of the classes they taught."

"I love that idea."

The air around Zoe shifted and a presence loomed at her side. She glanced up and met Haley Newton's blue eyes.

"Can I help you?" Zoe was unable to keep irritation from her voice.

"I just wanted to apologize to you," Haley said. She set two sundaes down on the table then gestured toward Chase, who still stood talking to the blond man. "I'm sure he told you."

Forcing herself to answer, Zoe said, "He did."

"Here we go," Mr. Kimmer said, setting two more pumpkin spice sundaes on the table and a small scoop of ice cream in a cup for Kylie and a cup of fresh fruit for Myles. "Thank you, young lady, for your help."

Haley smiled at him. "Not at all. You had your hands full."

"Thank you, Mr. Kimmer," Zoe said. "You are a good man."

He shrugged off her compliment. "Enjoy."

When Haley continued to stand there, Zoe gave a sigh. She was going to have to hear the woman out to get her to leave them alone. "Say your piece."

"Thank you," Haley said and took a seat across from Zoe in the booth.

"Should Myles and I leave?" Sadie asked.

"No, I'd rather you stayed," Zoe said.

"Yes, that would be great," Haley said at the same time.

"Here, Myles, eat a few bites of melon," Sadie encouraged her son before digging into her sundae.

Annoyance flashed in Haley's eyes.

Not in the least bit willing to accommodate the woman, Zoe prompted. "Well?"

"I'm really sorry for any pain I caused you," Haley said in an even tone. "I met Garrett when I took my car in to be fixed after I first arrived back in town. He hadn't been wearing a wedding ring. He flirted with me and asked me out. Now that I think about it, his insistence that we had to go to the next town over makes sense. At the time, I thought he was being chivalrous and wanting to take me to a fancy restaurant."

"Oh, that's him, chivalrous." The sarcasm was lost around a mouthful of pumpkin spice, caramel and nuts. Zoe really just wanted to enjoy her confection.

"Anyway," Haley said. "When I got the job at the hospital, and I met you and we became friends… I realized what an idiot I'd been. I broke things off with Garrett right away. I told him never to contact me again."

Zoe carefully put down her spoon and met Haley's gaze. "I accept your apology. This is on Garrett. He was a lousy husband

and even more of an immoral man. We are both better off without him."

The clearing of a throat brought all their gazes to Chase and Rocco standing next to the table.

"I've overstayed my welcome," Haley said. "Thank you, Zoe, for being such a generous person with your forgiveness."

Zoe didn't recall saying she'd forgiven the woman, but technically she forgave her. What she said was true, she blamed Garrett not Haley. But it would take time for the sour feelings to dissipate. She doubted she and Haley would ever be true friends again.

Haley slid from the booth and went to the counter where she grabbed a to-go bag presumably filled with ice cream. Zoe watched her leave as Chase and Rocco slid back into the booth.

"That was impressive," Chase said to her.

"Yes," Sadie joined in. "You were the epitome of grace."

If only that were true. Zoe couldn't say

she didn't still hold some bad feelings toward Haley, but eventually, she would get over it with God's help.

Her stomach twisted.

She ate a few more bites of her ice cream, which seemed only to upset her stomach more.

"Oh, look, there's Isla and her grandmother, Annette," Sadie said.

Zoe turned to see a dark-haired woman wearing jeans and a parka. Beside her, a shorter, older woman with gray hair stood in a long wool coat. Annette Jimenez was one of Zoe's clients.

Chase waved them over.

After paying for a to-go container of ice cream, Isla and her grandmother made their way over to the table.

"Ladies, would you care to join us?" Chase asked.

Annette waved off the offer. "We just stopped in to pick up a couple of sundaes. We have a holiday rom-com starting soon."

Isla smiled. "It's that time of year."

Everyone laughed. Zoe swirled her

spoon in the ice cream. A fuzzy sort of haze gripped her.

Chase leaned in close. "Would you be okay if I see Annette and Isla home, while you and Kylie stay here with Rocco and Sadie? You'll be safe."

Zoe blinked slowly. Though she understood his words, it took a moment to decipher them. With effort, she managed to say, "Oh. Sure. We'll be fine here."

He cocked his head. She smiled to reassure him. He nodded and told Rocco what he was doing. His voice sounded far away to Zoe, but she kept her gaze trained on the gooey mess she'd made of her ice cream. Beside her, Kylie banged her spoon on the table, the noise ricocheted through Zoe's brain.

Chase gently took the spoon from Kylie before he scooted out of the booth. "I'll be back in a jiff."

Dash rose and moved to his side.

Zoe watched Chase and Dash escort Isla and Annette through the crowded ice cream parlor and out the door.

Nausea roiled through Zoe's stomach. She turned to Rocco. "Would you mind grabbing to-go containers?"

"Grab me one, too," Sadie said. "This ice cream was very rich and too much for one sitting."

Rocco slid out of the booth.

"I feel bad for Isla," Sadie said.

Zoe stared at her friend and concentrated on forming words. "Annette told me Isla's been on the receiving end of some nastiness."

"Indeed," Sadie said. "I'm sure Chase just wants to make sure they get home safely."

Nodding, Zoe said, "He's a good man. I really like him." Did she slur her words? A pounding behind her eyes made her squint.

Sadie tilted her head. "Are you okay?"

"Upset stomach," Zoe replied with as much of a smile as she could muster. "Would you and Rocco walk me to Chase's house?"

"Of course." Sadie gathered her son and helped Zoe with Kylie.

"Ladies?" Rocco returned with the containers.

"I don't want the ice cream," Zoe said, swallowing back a bout of nausea. She hurried for the door with Kylie in her arms.

Outside, the cool air was a welcome relief. Zoe strapped Kylie into the stroller and nearly doubled over from the dizziness washing through her and the blood throbbing in her head.

"Everything okay?" Officer Steve asked as he came to her side.

Sweat beaded along Zoe's brow and down her back. Her hands began to shake. She headed for the nearest sidewalk bench where she could sit. She drew the stroller next to her, grateful to see Kylie had fallen asleep. Zoe wished she could go to sleep, then maybe the horrible sensations tearing through her would end.

Sadie sat beside her. "You don't look so good."

"I don't feel so good," Zoe said slowly. All the saliva in her mouth dried up. The world started to tilt. No, it was her. She listed sideways, slowly crumbling onto the bench. She could hear panic in Sadie's voice, but she couldn't make out the words as her vision tunneled into a black hole.

As they walked, Chase was aware that Dash kept looking back, as if he, too, hated leaving Zoe and Kylie's side. Chase was confident Rocco and Cocoa would protect the pair along with Sadie and her son, Myles. There was no reason to be concerned. He hoped Zoe didn't feel abandoned by him. He would explain to her later why he felt the need to make sure Isla and Annette made it safely home. He'd made a promise to himself to keep an eye on Isla and to help her however he could.

This past summer someone had done a hatchet job on the tech analyst's reputation, and had prevented her from adopting a little boy. Then someone had burned down Isla's home in an attempt to kill her. Isla was like family, as were all the Mountain Country K-9 Unit team members.

"That's strange," Annette said, breaking into Chase's thoughts.

"What is?" Chase asked.

They had just turned down the drive to Annette's home.

"I'm sure we left the porch light on," Isla said. "It must have burned out."

Caution tripped up Chase's spine as they gathered on the front porch. He reached up to test the light. Hot to the touch like a blub would be when it burned out. Still, he couldn't shake the wariness prickling his skin.

Chase held out his hand. He could just make out Isla and Annette in the ambient moonlight. "Let me clear the house."

Isla handed over the house key. Chase fitted the key in the lock and opened the door.

Dash growled and turned to face behind them. Alarm tightened Chase's muscles and his hand went to his sidearm.

"I have a gun trained on you so no sudden moves." The female voice came from a shadow near the bottom of the stairs.

Annette gasped.

Chase moved to shield Isla and her grand-mother. "Who's there?"

"Everyone, step inside," the woman de-manded.

Unsure what he was dealing with, Chase nudged Isla and Annette inside. He tight-ened his hold on Dash's leash, tugging the dog with him inside the house.

Could this be the person who had tried to ruin Isla's chances of adopting? The same person who had burned down Isla's house on the other side of town?

The same person responsible for blow-ing up Zoe's house? Did the two women have the same enemy?

The questions rattled around inside his mind like bees in a trap.

Isla flipped on the lights as they moved farther into the house.

The dark-hooded intruder followed them inside.

Isla gasped. "Lisa?"

Chase didn't recognize the woman with

stringy blond hair and a sharp nose, but, apparently, Isla did.

"Didn't think you'd see me again?" Lisa's voice held a note of malice.

"What are you doing here?" Isla asked, her voice shaking as she stepped in front of her grandmother. "Why do you have a gun?"

Lisa's face twisted with pain. "Because of you, my brother is gone."

Brother? Chase had no clue about the drama unfolding around him. "Isla, tell me what's happening?"

Isla made eye contact with Chase. "Lisa, her younger brother and I were in a foster home together when I was a teen," she explained. "Her brother ran away and apparently, she blames me. But it wasn't my fault."

"Liar!" Lisa shrieked.

"Whoa, stay calm," Chase said. "We can talk this through."

Isla focused on Lisa. "I covered for *you*."

"You were supposed to be watching us."

Lisa waved the gun. Her finger was on the trigger.

Chase's stomach clenched. "Ladies, please—"

Ignoring him, Lisa yelled at Isla. "You let him run away."

"I was making dinner. He took off because *you* were being mean to him," Isla's voice held a hard note that Chase had never heard from her.

"No!" Lisa screamed, her agitation ratcheting up. "You're responsible. You should have intervened. You were in charge."

"Isla." Chase caught her gaze again and shook his head, hoping she'd get the message and not let the woman get to her.

Isla visibly reined in her own upset. "I know it's hard for you to accept responsibility," Isla said gently. "You really need to get some help."

"Don't say that!" Lisa let out a shriek that shuddered through Chase.

"How did you find me?" Isla asked.

Chase eased his hold on Dash's leash, ready to drop the lead. He wouldn't give

Dash the command to attack while Lisa's finger was on the trigger. He hoped to find another way to defuse the situation.

"Lisa, I understand you're upset," Chase tried reasoning with her. "But this isn't the way to solve your problem. We can help you find your brother. If we work together."

She steadied the gun's barrel on Chase. "You don't know anything. You can't even capture the RMK."

Chase wasn't surprised she knew who he was. He hated that her words were true.

Keeping the gun trained on him, Lisa said, "I saw the news reporting on the Rocky Mountain Killer." Her gaze turned to Isla. "I saw you were part of the team investigating. I've been in town for months."

Isla spread her hands. "What do you want?"

Sneering, Lisa said, "Old granny, here, likes to talk to the ladies at the beauty place. It was no secret you were trying to adopt a child." Lisa's eyes darkened. "You shouldn't raise a child. You're nothing and deserve to be alone like me."

Shock crossed Isla's face. "You're the one who tanked my reputation with the child protective services?" Anger reverberated through her voice.

"They had to know what an awful person you are," Lisa insisted.

Shaking her head, Isla asked, "Did you also set fire to my house?"

Lisa cackled, a strange sort of laugh that was strangled by a cough. "It's just too bad you didn't die in that fire."

Chase had heard enough. He couldn't allow this unhinged woman to hurt Isla or Annette. Chase dropped Dash's leash, knowing the well-trained dog would stay put until commanded otherwise.

"Lisa, if you know who I am, you know I'm FBI," Chase said as he stepped forward, aware that the business end of the handgun she held was aimed at his chest. "You need to drop your weapon and surrender."

She scoffed. "Right. You're in no position to demand anything. I'm in control here."

Dash growled and then let out a series of ear-piercing barks.

Lisa seemed confused by the ruckus, which allowed Chase to tackle her. The gun Lisa held went off, the bullet embedding itself in the wall several feet from Isla.

Chase wrested the gun from Lisa's hand and flipped her onto her stomach to handcuff her.

Dash sniffed the woman as Chase holstered his weapon. Dash didn't alert to indicate there was any trace of explosives on her person.

Isla quickly called 911.

Within a short time, several police officers converged on the house and took Lisa into custody.

Chase and Dash moved to Isla and Annette. "Are you okay?"

Isla had her arms around her grandmother. "We are now. I can't believe it. Lisa is the one who's been harassing me and set the fire at my house. She blames me for her brother running away."

"At least now we know," her grandmother said.

"Yes," Chase agreed. "Having her in custody will go a long way to repairing the damage she's done to you, Isla."

Two Elk Valley police officers led Lisa out as she screamed obscenities at Isla. Chase would question her later when she'd calmed down to determine if she was involved in any way with the explosion at Zoe's house. But he had a feeling she wasn't.

Chase's phone rang. The caller ID showed Rocco's number. He answered. "Hey."

"It's Zoe. She's been taken to the hospital."

ELEVEN

Chase raced out of Isla's house and back to Main Street where he found Rocco, Cocoa, Sadie and the children.

"Go," Rocco said. "We'll take care of Kylie."

Chase stared at his task force member, his mind running through the possible reasons why Zoe had been taken to the hospital.

He should have stayed with her. Guilt nearly suffocated him. But he'd been in a hard place, having to decide whether to stick with Zoe or see Isla and Annette home. Chase had been confident Zoe would be safe with Rocco and Sadie. "What happened? I don't understand."

"She just collapsed," Sadie said. She had

both strollers in front of her. Kylie was sleeping.

Chase's heart thumped against his rib cage like a battering ram. "Is Kylie okay?"

Sadie's eyes widened. A silent oh formed on her lips. "I think so."

Chase quickly bent down and jostled Kylie, wanting to make sure the little nine-month-old woke up. Dash stuck his face inside the stroller to sniff Kylie. Kylie's eyes fluttered and she stretched. When her gaze focused on Chase's face, she smiled and babbled happily. Her gaze shifted to Dash and her little hands waved, trying to reach him.

Something inside of Chase gave way and a sob nearly escaped. This little girl had become so important to him. As important as her mother, Zoe. The realization had his breath catching. Now was not the time to examine the depths of his feelings for Zoe.

Not wanting to take any chances that Kylie had been harmed by whatever had happened to Zoe, Chase straightened and said, "We need to get to the hospital. All of us. I want Kylie to be looked at."

"We'll take our vehicle," Rocco said. "Kylie's stroller converts into a car seat."

"Lead the way," Chase said, anxious to get on the move, to get to Zoe. To find out what happened. If she died on his watch, he would never, ever forgive himself. He couldn't let another person he cared about perish because of his inability to protect them.

Thankfully, Rocco had brought his official Elk Valley PD vehicle to town. They loaded the dogs in the back compartment and the children in the back passenger seat with Sadie squeezed in between the two car seats. Chase jumped into the front passenger seat even though he wanted to take control of the SUV and drive. With lights and sirens blazing, they made quick time to the hospital.

Chase unbuckled and jumped out, released the locks holding Kylie's car seat in place and hurried into the hospital emergency room reception area. He skidded to a halt at the front desk.

"Zoe Jenkins," he said, his breath coming out in a huff. "I have her daughter. Kylie Jenkins. She needs to be seen. Call Dr. Webb, her pediatrician."

The nurse held up a hand. "Whoa, slow down. Is Kylie in distress?"

Chase looked down at the baby snug inside the car seat. Her wide trusting eyes stared up at him. His gut clenched with even more guilt and anxiety. This little girl needed her mother. This little girl had needed Chase to make sure her mother was safe. And he'd failed.

"I don't know," he finally said. "She seems okay. But her mother—"

"Zoe Jenkins has been taken to a room," the nurse said. "Let's have our ER doctor take a look at Kylie and then we'll go from there."

It took all of Chase's willpower not to rush to wherever they had taken Zoe. But right now, Zoe would want him to make Kylie the priority.

"I understand we have a little patient that might need some help?" a young female doctor said as she approached with a smile. She had long red hair held back in a braid down her back. Her white doctor's coat had the name Dr. Yvette Stinson stitched on the breast pocket. A stethoscope hung around her neck.

"Something happened to her mother, and I just want to make sure that she's okay," Chase said in a rush.

Yvette nodded with a kind smile as she bent forward to coo at Kylie. When she straightened, the doctor said, "Follow me. We'll go to exam room two."

Chase stayed right on the doctor's heels. Impatience threaded through his system and worry churned in his gut. He needed Kylie to be okay. He needed Zoe to be okay. Dr. Stinson indicated for Chase to set the car seat on the exam table, and then she proceeded to listen to Kylie's heart.

Chase paced as the doctor did a thorough exam.

He heard Rocco and Sadie talking outside the exam room. He opened the door and said, "Come in."

Sadie, Rocco and Myles crowded into the room, along with Dash. Rocco put his hand on Chase's shoulder and handed him his partner's leash. Chase gazed at Dash as more guilt flooded his system. In the rush to get Kylie into the hospital, Chase had neglected to release his dog from Rocco's vehicle. It was so unlike him. He'd make it up to Dash later with an extra chew bone. "Thank you for looking after him."

Rocco squeezed Chase's shoulder. "Of course."

"Kylie seems perfectly healthy," Dr. Stinson said. "Dad, you can take her home. She's fine."

The moniker of dad slashed over his heart. Rather than clarify his relationship to Kylie, he simply said, "Thank you, Doctor."

Sadie was at his side. "We'll stay with Kylie," she said. "If we need you, we'll have them page you. Go. Find out about Zoe. I need to know my friend is okay."

Having the reminder that Sadie and Zoe were friends helped Chase relinquish Kylie into Sadie's capable hands.

Dash nudged Chase as if to prod him into movement. Chase gave Rocco a grateful nod and hustled back to the nurses' station with Dash trotting alongside him. "Zoe Jenkins' room?"

"She's on floor three, room three-ten. I'll have the doctor meet you there," the nurse said.

With a sharp nod, Chase and Dash headed for the staircase, not wanting to wait for the elevator. They took the stairs two at a time to the third floor. They found room three-ten quickly. Taking a deep breath to calm his racing heart and to school his features into what he hoped was a neutral expression, Chase pushed open the door. He steeled himself against what he might find on the other side.

An awful beeping sound every few seconds disrupted Zoe from a deep, dreamless sleep. For some reason, she didn't want to come up from a state of unconsciousness. There seemed to be a war raging in her mind. She wanted to go back to that deep, dark abyss and yet, the incessant beeping drew her forward, until her senses gave way to awareness.

The scratchy feel of sheets on her skin made her restless. Her head tilted at an odd angle on a flat pillow. Uncomfortable from head to toe, slowly she rolled her neck and winced as the muscles protested. She swallowed, grimacing at the tender pain in her throat. Her mouth was dry. Her lips cracked. Light penetrated her eyelids. Instinctively knowing the brightness would sting her retinas, she scrunched up her eyes, wanting to hold off the inevitable.

Kylie!

The thought slammed into her as if someone had taken a fist to her jaw.

Her eyes jerked open, ignoring the painful way the sunlight streaming through the window to her right caused her eyes to water. She attempted to sit up. Her body refused to cooperate.

"Zoe, it's okay," the soft masculine voice soothed her.

Her gaze sought the source of that voice. She knew who it would be before he came into view. Chase. His expression was carefully blank, but she could see the worry in his dark eyes. He was trying so hard to be stoic. Didn't the man realize he could trust her with his heart?

She nearly laughed out loud at the stray thought, considering she had been resistant to trusting him with her heart. "Kylie?"

"Safe and healthy," Chase told her. "I had the ER doc check her over. Just in case. But she has a clean bill of health. She's with Sadie, Rocco and Myles. They will take good care of her."

Relief swept through her, bringing a wave of dizziness. She closed her eyes again, riding out the ebb until her stomach settled and the spinning in her head dissipated. "What happened?"

"We're still trying to figure that out," Chase said. "What do you remember?"

"I got up from the booth at the ice cream

parlor and suddenly didn't feel well. By the time I made it outside, I felt woozy and nauseous. I was struggling to breathe."

Chase's jaw hardened. She could tell he was debating with himself how much to reveal.

She frowned. "Tell me the truth. Don't sugarcoat it. I can't stand that."

For a moment his eyes closed. When he opened them, there was no mistaking his anger. "Someone tried to kill you. The doctors found fentanyl in your system."

Her breath stalled. "That's not possible. Is it? How?"

"We don't know. The team is working to figure it out. I don't want to jump to any conclusions until we have some answers. The paramedics gave you Narcan. If they hadn't—" His voice broke and he turned away.

Her heart stuttered at his display of emotion and the meaning behind his words. She would have died without the lifesaving drug used to reverse opioid overdoses.

Seeming to gain control of his emotions,

he faced her and cleared his throat. "I'm thankful you weren't alone. Sadie called for help quickly."

Her gaze jumped to the BP monitor that had started beating faster the moment she woke up. "I need to get out of here."

"Let me find the doctor and see what we can do," Chase said.

Sudden panic had Zoe reaching for him. He grasped her hand. "Don't leave me. You can use the call button."

He nodded and reached for the button hanging over the side railing of the hospital bed.

It took another hour for the doctor to release her into Chase's care. In the emergency room waiting area she was reunited with Kylie, as Chase pushed the wheelchair.

Kylie squealed with delight as Sadie picked her up and deposited her into Zoe's arms.

Liam Rawlston walked in with a big smile on his face. "Young lady, you gave us quite the scare."

"Certainly not my intention," Zoe said back to him with a small smile.

"Your chariot awaits," Liam said. He met Chase's gaze. "Are you coming home with us?"

"I am," Chase said. "I'll meet with the team in the morning."

Zoe craned her neck to the side and looked up at Chase. "I'll be fine with your dad and Officer Steve."

"You will," he agreed. "Tomorrow."

His voice was adamant, and she decided not to argue. She didn't in fact want him to leave her. He made her feel safe and cared for. She should rebel against letting a man take care of her, but for now she was going to let the Rawlston men continue to protect her and Kylie. Because obviously the person trying to kill her was not giving up.

"Here you go, boss." Ian handed Chase a set of keys after entering the conference room serving as the Mountain Country K-9 Unit hub in the Elk Valley police station.

It was the morning after Zoe had been

hospitalized, and Chase was having a hard time concentrating on what he needed to be doing. From the moment the doctor had told him that Zoe had fentanyl in her system, self-recriminations had been hounding him like dogs on the scent of fresh meat.

He took the keys and stuffed them into his pocket. "Any trouble?"

"None at all." Ian had just returned from Utah where he'd procured Trevor Gage's work truck so that Chase could impersonate Trevor. Ian moved around the conference room table and took a seat next to Meadow. "Trevor had left one of his company vehicles in the parking lot of his business. The keys were under the driver's seat like he said."

From the monitor on the wall, Trevor spoke. "I do have loyal employees."

"And the Stetson?" Chase asked.

"On the front seat waiting for you," Ian said.

The plan to convince the RMK that Trevor was back in town was coming together.

Bennett had rented a house in Trevor's name on the outskirts of town. And had mentioned to the management company that Trevor Gage was returning for the reunion. The hope was through the town's very active chatter among the residents, somehow the news would land in the serial killer's ear.

Rocco, sitting at the conference room table, filled the team in about the intruder at Isla's grandmother's home the night before. "Apparently, Isla was in foster care with Lisa and Bobby King. Both were younger than Isla. One night when the foster parents went out, leaving Isla in charge, the boy, Bobby, ran away. He was never seen again. Lisa blames Isla and was trying to ruin Isla's life."

"Any chance this Lisa King is working with the RMK?" Kyle asked from his seat across the table from Rocco.

Next to him, Ophelia shook her head. "I don't think so. She isn't from Elk Valley. I've gone through her financials, and with Isla's help we have dug into Lisa's past.

There is nothing to indicate she's working with the Rocky Mountain Killer."

"Could she have anything to do with the explosion at Zoe's house?" Meadow asked, swinging her gaze from Chase to Ophelia.

"Not that we can surmise," Ophelia said. "Also Dr. Webb's car was clean. Too clean. Whoever stole it wiped every inch down. I also searched the ice cream parlor for any traces of fentanyl and came up empty. No evidence to follow there."

"A fentanyl overdose didn't just happen out of the blue," Chase said. "Someone had to have managed to slip the drug into her system." Dr. Webb would have access to the drug. He came over to talk to Zoe. As did Haley Newton. His gut twisted with frustration and anger. "I need you all to help me figure this out."

Someone out there wanted to kill Zoe. Chase was going to do everything in his power to prevent them from succeeding.

The meeting broke up and Chase returned to his office. The stress from the past few days weighed heavy on his shoulders. He was doing what he could to capture the Rocky Mountain Killer by pretending to be Trevor. He really hoped this ruse worked.

Finding the person after Zoe was going to be more difficult. The perpetrator was smart and seemed to be a step ahead of them, which suggested it had to be someone close. Someone keeping tabs on Zoe and Kylie. But who?

Elk Valley wasn't a big city nor was it a tiny town. The residents all knew each other. Was it someone who didn't want the reunion to happen? Why? Was that someone helping the RMK? Or did they fear the RMK would show up, and this was their way of thwarting the event? Only a few people outside the task force and the police chief knew that Chase had received a text from the killer stating he was in town and planning to off Trevor at the reunion. His father. And Zoe.

But the information could have been leaked. He trusted his team. He trusted his father. And no way would Zoe have

said anything. None of them would deliberately reveal the information, but a slip of
the tongue was always a possibility. Or a
local police officer could have overheard
a conversation not meant for their ears.

Rubbing the back of his neck to relieve
some tension, he decided there was something he could do to make Isla's life better.

He had a few important phone calls to
make. At least this was one case wrapped
up. Now he had to solve the others once
and for all.

Going stir-crazy, Zoe was more than
ready to leave the Rawlston home and
meet with the reunion committee to go
over seating arrangements and the agenda.
The crisp fall air seeped under the collar of
her coat. She tucked a fuzzy white blanket
snugger around Kylie in the stroller. Her
baby waved a stuffed giraffe in her chubby
hand. Love swelled within Zoe's chest.

Kylie was her everything.

Blowing out a breath, Zoe pushed the
stroller down the street to the heart of Elk

Valley with the town hall as their final destination. Beside her, Liam ambled along in a navy peacoat and jaunty hat covering his gray hair. Officer Steve and Meadow followed close behind, providing protection, and Zoe tried to relax.

For the past three days, the Elk Valley High School reunion committee had met via video conferencing, text and email. It wasn't ideal but it seemed to work. After today's meeting at the town hall ballroom where they were holding the reunion, Zoe and Sadie would convene at Sadie's catering kitchen so that they could work together on the menu.

The honk of a horn drew her attention to a big black truck with the logo of Gage Ranch Consulting on the side panel door. The man driving wore a silver Stetson, pulled low as to shield his face, presumably from the late October sunlight cutting through the trees lining the street. He gave a short wave as he drove past. To the pedestrians on the street, it would look as if Trevor Gage was back in town.

Zoe smiled softly and lifted a hand in greeting…to Chase, who she knew was behind the wheel of the truck. He wasn't happy that she had insisted on this in-person meeting at the town hall, but the reunion was in two days, and they needed to finalize preparations. She'd already sent ahead the projects she'd worked on while holed up at the Rawlston's. She'd decorated framed photos of various high school events throughout the years, and she made centerpieces for the tables using candles and foliage picked from Liam and Chase's backyard.

Arriving at the town hall made Zoe breathe a little easier. They made it in one piece. She hadn't realized how stressed she was on the trek over. But lately, stress seemed to be a constant companion. Except when Chase was around. His calm demeanor and steady presence anchored her in ways she'd never experienced with anyone else. She admired him so much. His dedication to his team, to the town, and to her and Kylie. He was a man of integrity and worthy of her respect.

Affection spread through her, and she knew if she weren't careful she could fall for him. She was already becoming too dependent on him, letting her heart get involved would only make her vulnerable to heartache, a state of being she didn't relish or want to experience again.

The decorating team had already started transforming the large room into a glitzy walk down memory lane. Sadie rushed forward when she saw Zoe.

As she absorbed Sadie's hug, Zoe realized how isolated she had become during her marriage. Garrett had demanded all of her attention and time. In the months after her divorce, she'd felt shamed by her failure and had kept to herself outside of the hospital and her clients.

Though she and Sadie had always been friendly, she would've categorized their relationship as more of acquaintances. But now she was thankful to say that she counted Sadie as a good friend.

"Here, let me take Kylie while you go do your thing," Liam said.

She released her hold on the stroller and gave the man a quick hug. His aftershave smelled nice, comforting. She was grateful to have him in her life. "You're the best," she told him.

With a chuckle, Liam pushed the stroller away to where a group of children ranging in age from five to preteen, who belonged to other committee members, were playing duck, duck, goose.

For a moment, Zoe watched the group with an ache in her heart. One day Kylie would be that age. Time was flying by so fast. She could only pray she'd live long enough to see her daughter grow up. But after three attempts on her life, she wouldn't feel safe until Chase caught the person targeting her.

Why did someone want her dead? The unfathomable reason proved elusive and added to her stress.

Linking her arm through Zoe's, Sadie said, "Let's make this happen."

Taking a breath to clear her nerve-racking thoughts, Zoe focused on the ballroom and making the reunion the best social event of the town's history.

After parking Trevor's truck at the Elk Valley Park and walking down the street and into the police station, Chase entered his office and removed the Stetson hat from his head. He also traded out a jean jacket for his FBI jacket, then headed to the training center where he'd left Dash this morning with the task force dog trainer, Liana Lightfoot.

Liana had worked for the county before Chase had recruited her to work with the task force. She was excellent at training in all disciplines of the working K-9, as well as therapy service dogs.

When he entered the training ring, he found Dash surrounded by Cowgirl's four puppies. He was confounded by the fact that the serial killer they were after had been decent enough to turn over the labradoodle puppies because he couldn't take care of them. Chase really hoped Cowgirl was faring well.

Chase allowed himself a few moments to just enjoy Dash being a regular dog. But soon Dash lifted his nose, turned his head and spotted him. Jumping over a couple of puppies, Dash raced to the edge of the ring. The puppies followed the big golden retriever, their happy yips echoing off the training room walls. Liana joined him outside the gate.

"Aren't they so cute?" she asked. She was a tall and fit woman with a warm disposition and was devoted to the dogs. Her long dark hair hung down her back and her dark eyes followed the puppies.

"Very," Chase agreed. His heart squeezed with tenderness. He loved dogs. Most K-9 officers did, or they wouldn't become K-9 handlers.

Dash went up onto his hind legs and put his front paws on the gate. He was nearly as tall as Chase when stretched out. Dash stuck his nose toward Chase in greeting. Chase rubbed Dash behind the ears. The dog's tongue lolled to the side in a happy response. "I hope you're being nice to those little ones," he said to the dog.

Dash's plumed tail wagged vigorously in answer.

"He's a good boy," she said. "The young ones learn from the older ones as well as from formal training."

She handed Chase Dash's leash. "Any word on Cowgirl?"

Hating to disappoint her, Chase shook his head. "We can't lose hope."

"I keep praying she'll turn up," Liana said. "But with every passing day, it's harder to stay hopeful."

"I'll let you know the minute we hear anything," Chase promised.

After leashing up Dash, Chase said goodbye to Liana, and they left the police station. They walked down Main Street, Dash sniffing the cool air.

"Hey, boss," Rocco and his dog, Cocoa, fell into step beside him. "Are you headed to town hall?"

"I am," Chase said. "You?"

"Yep. Sadie's there with the committee decorating," he said. "Any more texts from the RMK?"

Heaving a sigh, Chase said, "No. But 'Trevor' has made several passes through town and stopped at the gas station where he gassed up."

Dash was at the end of the lead, his nose twitching. An unsettled sensation dropped to the pit of Chase's gut. What scent was the dog picking up?

"Kyle and Ian are camped out in the rented house," Rocco said.

"The trap has been set," Chase said. "Now, we just have to hope he takes the bait."

Chase's cell phone buzzed inside his jacket pocket. Still walking, he took the device out. He didn't recognize the number. He pressed the answer button. "Rawlston."

The sound of maniacal laughter filled his ears. Unease slithered down Chase's spine. Hadn't Zoe said she'd heard a weird sort of laughter before the bomb that destroyed her home exploded?

He halted and held the phone away from him, putting it on speaker so that Rocco could also hear.

"Who is this?" Chase demanded.

Suddenly, Dash started pulling, straining at the end of the lead, scrabbling on the sidewalk. He nearly pulled Chase off his feet. Sharing a concerned glance with Rocco, Chase unhooked Dash and the dog took off like a rocket. Chase ran after him with Rocco and his K-9 close on his heels. Keeping Dash in sight, Chase's stomach dropped when he realized Dash was headed straight for the town hall building.

The dog veered off to the right side of the building housing the event space and came to a skidding halt. He sat by the wall and barked.

"He's alerting!" Chase told Rocco. "Evacuate the premises."

Rocco and his dog peeled away and rushed inside the town hall entrance.

Chase rushed to Dash's side and quickly

attached his leash to his harness. Following the dog's gaze, Chase searched the ground on the side of the building. His gaze snagged on a patch of earth that had been disturbed near the outer wall beneath a window.

Going to his knees, the soft dirt squishing under his weight, he dug with his hands until he uncovered an explosive device.

His throat closed tight. Zoe and Kylie were in the building. So was his father. Sadie and others. They were all in danger. He couldn't let anything happen to them.

TWELVE

Heart hammering in his chest, Chase sat back on his heels in the soft dirt outside the town hall building. He grabbed his cell phone, and quickly called Ophelia, the task force's crime scene expert. "I need your help with an explosive device. Bring me the portable TVC."

Chase described the cylindrical canister with a cell phone strapped to the middle by duct tape. "It's buried just outside the south wall of the town hall ballroom. The device can be remotely detonated. And could have a long range."

"Are there people in the building? You need to evacuate. I'm on my way." Ophelia sounded like she was running.

"Rocco's on it." Chase glanced toward

the front of the building where a steady stream of people coming out of town hall flooded the sidewalk. He wanted to find Zoe, Kylie and his dad, but containing the device had to be his priority. The best way to protect everyone was to defuse the device before it detonated.

"I can disarm this thing," he said into the phone. "Stay with me."

"If you disturb the device, it might go off." There was no mistaking the concern lacing her words.

He considered the wisdom of her words. Better to be safe than sorry. He tugged on Dash's leash and backed away. He'd hoped the TVC—total containment vessel—he'd helped procure for the Elk Valley PD would never be required. But after the bombing that had devastated his life, having one available gave him peace of mind. Not that it would have helped in the situation with Elsie and Tommy. He hadn't been there to help them. No one had. They'd died alone. Leaving him grieving and broken.

But he was helping Zoe and the others now. He wouldn't let anyone else die. Not on his watch.

Chase's cell phone rang again. The number was unfamiliar. Just like the last call. Scanning the area for anything or anyone out of place, his gaze stalled. There by a tree in Elk Valley Park at the end of Main Street, he saw a hooded figure.

Afraid to answer the call on his phone in case it might trigger the bomb as Ophelia suspected, Chase kept his gaze trained on the suspicious person in the park.

Ophelia joined him on the sidewalk with the TVC in tow. The spherical core chamber sat on top of a wheeled cart.

He pointed to the figure who now raised a hand in the air. Was it the phone? "I think that's the bomber."

Ophelia followed his gaze. "If that's true, we don't have time to contain the bomb. We need to get these people as far away as possible."

"You do that. I'm going after the suspect." Chase ran toward the hooded figure with Dash at his side.

Behind him, the world exploded.

He and Dash were flung forward. He landed on the ground with a thud that reverberated through him. Dash let out a bark as he crashed to the ground, but the dog quickly regained his footing.

Getting to his hands and knees, Chase watched the hooded figure run in the opposite direction through the park, getting farther away.

"Boss! You okay?" Rocco and his dog rushed up.

Getting to his feet and shaking the residual effects of the explosion from his head, Chase sucked in a breath. "Casualties?"

"No. We cleared the building before the explosion," Rocco said. "Only structural damage."

Sending up a quick, thankful prayer, Chase said, "Come on. We can't let him get away."

They raced after the bomber, running through the park straight to the parking lot.

The fall leaves crunched beneath their feet and they slid on the slick, dewy ground.

With frustration, Chase watched the bomber jump into a silver truck, back up and speed away.

Unfortunately, Chase had left the keys to Trevor's truck, also parked in the Elk Valley Park parking lot, in the jean jacket in his office inside the Elk Valley police station. He'd never make it inside to grab the keys and back in time to follow the truck.

"That was Garrett Watson's company truck," Rocco said, his voice seething with anger.

Dismay and anger had Chase's hands fisting at his side. Garrett Watson had a lot to answer for.

"Was that the suspect?" Bennett and Spike, his beagle, raced to where Rocco and Chase stood in the parking lot of Elk Valley Park.

Containing his rage at Zoe's ex-husband, Chase said, "Rocco, Bennett, secure the scene. I'm going after Garrett."

"Not alone, you aren't," Bennett said, his

voice hard. Beside him, his dog sat waiting to go to work. Unfortunately, having
a narcotics detection dog in this instance
wasn't going to help them find Garrett.
"Meadow and Ophelia are on scene. I'm
going with you."

Chase could see the indecision on Rocco's face. "Rocco, go make sure Sadie and
Zoe and the kiddos are okay." He trusted
the man would protect the women and children with his life. "Get them to safety. And
my dad, too."

Without hesitation, Rocco nodded. He
and Cocoa hustled away, heading back to
the scene where smoke rose in dark spi-
rals of doom to the sky. Half of the town
hall ballroom was gone. Chase's stomach
twisted. Zoe would be so upset. He wanted
to go to her, to comfort her, but his first
priority had to be bringing in Garrett Watson. The man would pay for terrorizing
and attempting to kill his ex-wife.

Chase, Dash, Bennett and Spike hustled
to the police station where they piled into
an official Mountain Country K-9 Unit ve-

hicle. After securing their dogs in the back compartment, with Bennett at the wheel, they drove to the other side of town where Watson Motors was located.

The vehicle barely came to a halt before Chase jumped out and released Dash. Putting the dog on a long lead, Chase stomped toward the entrance. Bypassing the reception entrance, he entered the garage where several mechanics were working on various cars and trucks.

"Garrett Watson. Where is he?" He held up his FBI badge.

An older gentleman wearing blue coveralls smeared with grease walked over. "I haven't seen Garrett all day. I'm Fred Comet, I manage the shop for the Watsons. Can I help you with something?"

"If Garrett's not here, where would he be?" Chase asked.

"I couldn't rightly say," Fred said. "But you could check out his parents' place. They live off Tiburon Road. The last I heard, old man Watson and his wife were traveling."

Chase clenched his jaw and spun on his heel. He wasn't going to take the man's word at face value. "Search," he told Dash.

The dog went into working mode, his nose twitched and lifted in the air. He started a slow procession through the garage, sniffing the workers without alerting on them. Dash moved on quickly, clearing the garage, supply closets and reception area without alerting.

Okay, maybe Garrett wasn't building his bombs here at the garage but maybe he was at his parents' home. Meeting back up with Bennett outside, Chase said, "Nothing."

"Ditto," Bennett said. "I talked to everyone. Nobody has seen Garrett today."

"We need to put out a BOLO on his truck," Chase said. He loaded Dash back into the Mountain Country K-9 Unit vehicle.

Bennett nodded and loaded his dog in the back as well.

After climbing into the driver's seat, Bennett started the engine, while Chase grabbed the dashboard radio to call in about Garrett's silver four-by-four truck with the Watson Motors logo on the sides.

The dispatch operator said, "Hold on one second." There was a moment of silence before she came back on. "Garrett Watson reported that truck stolen this morning." The dispatcher rattled off the address for his parents' Elk Valley home.

"Convenient," Chase said, not for one second believing that Garrett's vehicle had been stolen but rather that Garrett had reported it as such to cover his tracks.

Bennett stepped on the gas, and they headed to the Watson property. When they arrived at the ranch-style house, Garrett Watson stepped out the front door. Paint peeled off the banister and dead flowers in window boxes drooped.

"Did you find my truck?" Garrett asked. "I assume that's why you've made the trek out here."

"I'll ask the questions," Chase said. "You're coming with us."

"Excuse me?" Garrett frowned and

crossed his arms over his chest. "You're taking me in? On what grounds?"

"On the grounds that you're suspected of blowing up the town hall building." Bennett stepped forward to grasp Garrett by the biceps. His dog stood beside him, his ears back.

"Whoa, now," Garrett said. "I don't know anything about any kind of explosions. I woke up this morning to find my truck was gone. My parents are off on a cruise now that Dad's retired. I had no way to get to town except walk, and well, that isn't happening. I'm not much for exercise."

"You can tell us all about it at the station," Chase said. "First, do I have your permission to search your property?"

"Search?" Garrett jerked away from Bennett. "What exactly are you looking for?"

"What you used to make a bomb," Chase told him.

Garrett laughed. He made a sweeping gesture with his arms. "Knock yourself out. I have nothing to hide."

Dislike for the man set Chase's nerves on edge. "We'll see."

Once again, Chase gave the command for Dash to search. They started with the outside perimeter of the house and the garage. With mounting frustration, Chase followed behind Dash while the dog continued on without alerting. They moved into the house. The odors of coffee and grilled onions turned Chase's stomach. But still Dash didn't alert.

Just because Garrett didn't build his devices at his workplace or his parents' home didn't mean he wasn't behind the attacks on Zoe. But Chase had to admit he had no cause to detain Garrett.

"Don't leave town," Chase told him.

Garrett scoffed with a careless shrug. "Until you find my truck, I have no wheels. I couldn't leave town even if I wanted to. I've already called the insurance company. It will be days before I can get a rental here."

Far from satisfied, Chase had to walk away even though everything inside of him wanted to punch the smirk off the man's face. Chase would find out how Garrett had arranged for the explosion. There was no doubt in his mind Garrett was guilty of something. He just didn't know what yet.

"I should have canceled the reunion the minute we knew the Rocky Mountain Killer was back in town." Zoe couldn't keep the self-recriminations from tainting her voice and betraying the guilt flooding her system. Her gaze went to Kylie in the playpen. She waved a toy in the air and then crawled to the edge of the pen and pulled herself to her feet.

They were safe now back in the Rawlston's home. Their sanctuary. Was it wrong of Zoe to never want to step outside again?

"This is not on you," Chase said.

He'd returned to the house several minutes ago and explained that her ex-husband's truck had been seen fleeing the site of the explosion. But he'd also explained they had no cause to arrest Garrett yet. It just was so awful.

"Sure, it's on me," she countered, tearing her gaze from Kylie to meet his. "There was so much opposition to begin with. Somebody doesn't want this reunion to happen. I should've heeded the signs."

"We don't know that this is the work of someone in town. Or the RMK. I still suspect it's Garrett," Chase told her.

"But you didn't find any evidence to suggest he was behind this," Zoe reminded him. "Innocent until proven guilty, correct?"

She could tell from the irritated expression marching across Chase's face that in his book Garrett was guilty and proving him innocent was going to be difficult in Chase's eyes.

She hated to think that Garrett hated her so much that he would try to kill her and other innocent people. What he was supposedly doing didn't make sense.

"True. But let's just take it one problem at a time," Chase said. "Right now, keeping you and Kylie safe is my priority."

His words seeped through her, making

her want to weep. Being someone's priority was a dream. Having someone to lean on and to spend her life with had led her into a disastrous marriage. But Chase was nothing like Garrett.

Chase was honorable and trustworthy.

And had a job to do. His priority should be stopping the Rocky Mountain Killer.

"I need to take Kylie and leave. That would be best for everyone," Zoe said. The idea took shape in her mind. "I should've done this to begin with. We can go visit my parents in Florida. The reunion will have to wait until—" She heaved a sigh. "Never. It was a selfish dream of mine to bring the town together."

A shudder ran through her as the memory of the explosion destroying town hall ricocheted through her mind, bringing back echoes of the explosion that had damaged her house. The fear of being evacuated, the terror of how close they all came to being caught in the blast crimped her chest.

"It was not selfish," Chase assured her.

"You were trying to do a good thing. And running isn't the answer." He moved to put an arm around her waist, the warmth of his presence chasing away the icy cold seeping through her veins.

She turned to face him, her hands going to his chest. His heart beat in a steady rhythm beneath her palms. Comforting and secure. "I wish I had half the self-confidence you do."

"Believe me, I'm as flawed and insecure as anybody," Chase said to her. "I'm just better at hiding my foibles. Zoe, listen to me." He tightened his hold on her. "You're not to blame for the actions of someone else. If this is truly about stopping the reunion, the person could have gone about it in a completely different way. But they chose destruction. And whoever did this will pay."

"I'm just so grateful to God that no one was hurt today." Emotions clogged her throat. The panic when Rocco came into the event hall, his voice reverberating off the walls, telling them to evacuate, still had her heart racing.

She'd been too far from Kylie to grab her. Thankfully, Liam had had her in his arms, and he'd reacted swiftly, carrying Kylie to safety.

Yet, the fear persisted. A shiver raced over her arms and down her spine. There could have been numerous fatalities, including children. The bomber had no conscience.

Chase rubbed her biceps. "You're cold."

"It's the letdown of the adrenaline from earlier," she told him but the fear that was never far away was also chilling her bones.

He nodded and drew her against him. She clung to him, to his strength. The lingering scent of the explosion filled her nostrils, along with the spicy masculine scent of his aftershave. It was a reminder that once again he'd saved her and everyone else's life. He was a true hero. She leaned back in his arms and looked up into his face. Words escaped her as she met his gaze. The dark depths were brimming with emotions that had her heart pounding against her rib cage, sending flutters of anticipation through her system.

Without stopping to question the sudden yearning compelling her to go on her tiptoes and slide her hands around his neck, she pulled him toward her mouth. Their lips met. He stiffened as if surprised, or was he resistant?

Mortification engulfed her. She'd overstepped. Misread the situation. Taken advantage of his kindness.

On the verge of breaking off the kiss, he softened, his arms tightening as he deepened the kiss, filling her senses with his masculinity. He tasted of safety and care. Her heart expanded and the knowledge that this man had become so important to her clamored through her mind and settled with a soft landing. She couldn't find any remorse for letting him into her heart.

Kylie's happy babbling brought Zoe back to reality. What was she doing? Becoming involved with Chase romantically would only leave her devastated in the end. She couldn't let him into her heart. She couldn't take another blow, especially when she had the very distinct feeling Chase could decimate her in ways that she'd never experienced.

Slowly, she eased away from Chase. "I'm sorry," she said. "I know you're not interested in me, and I don't know why I did that. It just…"

He brushed her hair back from her face, his touch gentle. He lifted her chin with his finger. "You don't have to apologize. The last few days have been traumatic in so many ways. I don't want to hurt you."

Too late.

Her heart ached with longing to belong to him and for them to be a family.

But she wouldn't tell him that. She hurt knowing that she and Kylie could never compete with the memory of his lost wife and child. And she was still reeling from having learned about Garrett's betrayals, more of which were coming to light even after their divorce. Was she latching onto Chase as a safe harbor when really what she needed to do was focus on herself and Kylie right now? Despite her efforts to avoid letting down her guard, somehow Chase had infused her heart with hope that maybe there was a chance for them. A pipe dream. She couldn't risk her heart again. Could she?

She placed her hand over his heart. "You're a good man. Now, it's time for Kylie and me to rest. I don't know how much more of this I can take."

He released his hold on her. She picked Kylie up and headed for the guestroom, shutting the door in time to keep Chase from seeing the floodgates open and the tears streaming down her face.

"Tell me you found something in the truck," Chase said to Ophelia the next morning.

News had come overnight that Garrett's silver truck had been found abandoned along the highway twenty miles outside of town. Ophelia had processed the vehicle before releasing it back to Garrett.

Chase had called a team meeting. Now they all crowded in the conference room again. He hated that it seemed they were spinning their wheels instead of gaining traction.

"Unfortunately, the truck had been wiped down. Exactly like Dr. Webb's car," Ophelia informed him and the rest of the task force. "Not even a stray hair."

"Whoever's behind this is very thorough and calculated," Ian said. He and Kyle had left the rental house they were using to pose as Trevor's in the care of officers from the Elk Valley PD to attend the meeting.

With the reunion now kaput, their plan to trap the Rocky Mountain Killer was on shaky ground. They couldn't let him leave town before they caught him. Chase had driven through town once again this morning, posing as Trevor Gage. But his efforts seemed futile. There hadn't been any more communication from the serial killer.

"Are we any closer to finding Evan Carr or Ryan York?" Chase tried to keep the vibration of frustration and irritation from showing, but he was doing a poor job of containing his emotions.

After the unexpected kiss last night that he had shared with Zoe, he'd had little rest. His mind played over his father's words telling him it was time to move on. To let his heart mend. Yet, he felt like he was taking advantage of Zoe in her moment of weakness. She was scared and flailing emotionally. Raising a child alone, then having someone destroying her house, try to run her over, poison her with a narcotic and then blowing up the town hall ballroom while she and Kylie were inside was enough to make anyone vulnerable enough to seek solace. Even solace in his arms. He couldn't let her make a mistake that she'd regret later. He needed to be stronger for both of them.

"We aren't any closer to discovering the whereabouts of Evan or Ryan than we were three days ago," Ashley informed him.

"They can't just have fallen off the face of the earth," Chase said. Turning his gaze to Isla, he said, "Have you tapped into all of the databases we have access to?"

She cocked her head and gave him a censoring look. "Of course, I have."

He held up a hand in apology. "I know, I know. Sorry." He ran a hand through his hair. "I don't mean to take my frustrations out on any of you."

"What do we make of Garrett Watson?" This from Trevor on the video monitor. He and Hannah sat side by side, their faces filling one half the screen. "I know you said he didn't have a knife tattoo on his forearm. But what if the knife tattoo had been a fake?"

"Unfortunately, Garrett has an alibi for the time that the Rocky Mountain Killer was seen in Idaho and in Utah," Selena said, from the other half of the monitor.

"I still think he's involved in the attempts on Zoe's life," Chase said. He didn't care if he was stubbornly clinging to that theory. He didn't like the man. And maybe that was coloring Chase's perspective. Garrett had shirked his responsibilities to Zoe and Kylie. The man wasn't trustworthy.

The door to the conference room opened. Police Chief Nora Quan stepped inside. Dressed impeccably in a tailored pantsuit in a deep plum color, the woman exuded authority and confidence. "I have some good news."

Chase perked up, hoping she would say they had a lead on Evan Carr or Ryan York, or some evidence to incriminate Garrett Watson. Something that would break their cases.

"Pastor Jerome has offered up the church's community room for the reunion," she said. "I've already informed Zoe and the reunion committee."

Chase's stomach sank. Not the news he was hoping for. "Another opportunity for the person trying to hurt Zoe to strike."

Nora leveled a finger at him, her gaze behind her glasses sharp. "I propose we go through with the reunion. The reunion itself will be heavily guarded. We continue to spread the word that Trevor will attend but then at the last moment, he decides not to for some reason. You, with your team, wait at the rental house for the Rocky Mountain Killer."

"But what about Zoe?" The question was out before Chase could filter the thought. His priorities had shifted to the woman who he was falling for. And he wasn't going to apologize.

"We will keep her under guard at your house," Nora said.

Chase couldn't argue with the plan. However, Zoe would balk. But knowing how guilty she felt for the town hall explosion, he hoped she would agree to let the reunion commence without her. It was the best way for him to do his job.

And the best way to protect her. If she were there, he didn't know if he could concentrate on the RMK when all he'd want to do was be by Zoe's side.

THIRTEEN

"What do you mean you want me to stay home?" Zoe stared at Chase. She couldn't have been more stunned than if he'd grown antlers and a shiny red nose.

She tucked her feet beneath her, the leather of the couch in the Rawlston's living room creaked with the movement. Chase sat opposite her in an arm chair with his hands on his knees and his intense gaze pinning her in place.

The fact that he was echoing the thought she'd had when the police chief had called with the news about using the church community room for the reunion didn't make hearing the words coming from Chase's mouth any easier to absorb.

Chase winced. "I know it's not ideal.

But after what happened at the town hall, I think it would be best if you didn't attend the reunion."

"You think it would be best," she repeated with a dull ache pounding beneath her breastbone. It was one thing for her to decide not to go and a completely different issue for him to say she shouldn't go.

Because he thought it would be best.

How many times had Garrett made a decree, claiming he knew better than her? Too many to count. She hadn't recognized his chauvinism until long after they'd married. She'd mistaken his need to be in control and to make the decisions as his way of caring for her. Was she making that same mistake with Chase?

"I'm just saying..." Chase held his hands up in a gesture of surrender. "If you were the target of the bombing, and we have to assume you were, then maybe it would be better if you didn't go. Safer for everyone. Especially you and Kylie. You are my only concern."

Irritation and guilt swamped her. He

was nothing like Garrett. He'd proven that over and over. He was a man of honor and integrity. A protector and a gentleman. Her shoulders slumped. "You're right, of course. I'm being silly. I shouldn't attend."

"Not silly," he countered. "The reunion is your project. I hate that you'll have to miss it. If I could be in two places at once, I'd go with you and keep you safe."

And he would. She didn't doubt it for a moment. But it was more important for him to stop the serial killer terrorizing the town than for her be at the reunion. "I can coordinate with Sadie as much as possible so that she's not left with all the responsibility."

"That's perfect." Chase's voice was filled with relief. "I'm sure she would appreciate your thoughtfulness."

"At least somebody does," Zoe groused and immediately regretted her words.

She knew it wasn't fair to be taking her upset out on Chase. He was only trying to protect her. That's what he did. Protected people. Her heart rate ticked up at the thought of what his job might cost him. When she'd come out of the town hall building, she'd seen Chase running through the park and had sent up prayers that he would be safe, more than a little concerned for him.

It was hardly fair for her to begrudge him the same concern.

She needed to trust that God had all of them in his hands.

But that wouldn't stop her from worrying about Chase.

She sent up a silent prayer for God to suppress her growing affection for the man. But that was becoming harder with every passing moment. Especially since she knew he was going to continue with his plan to impersonate Trevor Gage and hopefully lure the Rocky Mountain Killer into a trap. It was dangerous.

Chase was putting his life on the line for them all.

"I'm sorry. You don't deserve my snark," she said, contrition making her wince. "I'm just frustrated."

"As long as you're safe, I'll take any snark you want to throw my way. I can handle it," he replied in a husky voice that sent a ribbon of affection and admiration through her.

He wasn't the type of man to take offense or be too sensitive of criticism. She really liked that about him.

Her staying home, safe with Meadow and Officer Steve standing guard, would help Chase stay focused on what he needed to do.

She sent up a silent prayer that Chase would come through this unscathed and the Rocky Mountain Killer would be caught.

Chase left his house wearing his Mountain Country K-9 Unit uniform of light gray jacket and slacks, secure in the knowledge that between Meadow, her K-9 partner Grace, and Officer Steve, Zoe and Kylie would be well protected. His dad was also staying home, too, since he had not graduated from Elk Valley High School, having moved to Elk Valley in his mid-twenties for a job with the fire department.

Chase carried a duffel bag containing Trevor's silver Stetson and one of his company logo jackets to his Mountain Country K-9 Unit vehicle. He opened the back compartment for Dash to jump in.

Earlier in the day, he'd parked Trevor's truck at the church and walked away wearing his Trevor disguise. So now when he reached the church parking lot, he brought the vehicle to a halt next to Trevor's truck.

Leaving Dash comfortable and safe in his compartment, Chase entered through the main entrance. He stopped by the welcome table to grab his and Trevor's name tags. Peeling off the back of the stickered name tag, he placed his own name on the breast pocket of his uniform while tucking Trevor's name tag into his pocket.

Moving farther into the church's community room, located below the sanctuary, he scanned the space. Tables had been set up all around with donated and borrowed tableware. There wasn't much in the way of decorations since everything Zoe and her committee had used to decorate the town hall ballroom had been destroyed. He noted the gathering was rather small, consisting mostly of first responders, who were local to Elk Valley and a few old-timers like Mr. Kimmer from the ice cream parlor and his wife.

Rocco approached. He'd left his K-9 partner at home as well.

"Not a big turnout," Chase commented.

"Honestly, I think most people are skittish about attending, seeing as the last venue was blown up and all," Rocco said, with a wry twist of his lips.

Sadie joined them, linking her arm through Rocco's. "This will be a dry run. We'll do another reunion, maybe next year."

"Zoe will be happy to hear that," Chase said.

"It was her idea."

Chase wasn't surprised. The woman was always thinking ahead. One of the many reasons he admired and respected her. She was a strong and capable woman who was also thoughtful and kind. He didn't like being here without her.

Stay on task, he silently reminded himself.

"I hear that Trevor has made an appearance," Sadie said loudly. "Someone said he wasn't feeling well and is in the bathroom."

Chase appreciated Sadie's help. He scanned the room again. Ashley and her husband, Cade McNeal, along with Cade's younger sister, Melissa, stood talking with Jessie Baldwin from the Rusty Spoke.

"I'll go check on Trevor," Chase said and strode away.

He stopped to say hello to Ashley and her family. Raising his voice to ensure he was overheard by the other attendees, he said, "I was going to check on Trevor in the restroom. Sounds like he might have a little bit of food poisoning."

"Oh, that's horrible," Ashley said. "Let us know if we can help."

After making a show of checking the

bathroom, Chase returned to say loudly, "Trevor went out the side door and is headed back to his rental. He's pretty sick."

Ashley and Cade helped spread the word around the reunion space. With a nod of appreciation to Ashley, Chase walked out of the church into the parking lot.

Careful to stay out of the overhead lights, he stepped between Trevor's truck and his vehicle. After opening the truck's passenger door, he used the remote for his K-9 unit vehicle to release Dash. The dog quickly made the transition from the K-9 unit to the truck.

"Floor," Chase murmured to Dash. The dog settled on the floorboard, his head resting on the bench seat.

Placing Trevor's Stetson on his head, Chase closed the door and walked around the back end of the truck.

The sensation of being watched had the fine hairs on the back of his neck quivering.

He sent up a quick prayer that Dash hadn't been seen.

Marveling at how easy praying was once again becoming, Chase started Trevor's truck and backed out of the parking spot. He pulled down the visor, hoping to help shield his face from view. Driving down Main Street slowly so anyone watching would think Trevor was at the wheel, Chase kept an eye on his rearview mirror for a tail while also scanning the alleys of the business he passed, searching for any signs of a threat.

His cell phone dinged.

He waited until he was out of town before fishing the cell phone out of his front jeans pocket. Checking for signs of another vehicle and seeing none, he pulled to the edge of the road to read the text. The number was blocked. Adrenaline spiked through his veins.

Poor Trevor! Food poisoning will be the least of his worries when I'm done with him. Sorry, you won't reach him in time even if you leave the reunion now.

With a growl, Chase tossed the phone onto the bench seat. Aloud he said, "Bring it on."

Dash made a noise in his throat as if in agreement.

Pulling the truck back onto the road, Chase sped to the rental house. The two-lane road was quiet and dark. No headlights behind him but that didn't mean a vehicle wasn't back there, staying in the shadows. Foreboding gripped his gut. The houses on this side of town were spaced out with long driveways. He turned down the one for the rental house.

The ranch-style house with its low-pitched roof and large windows stood dark at the end of the lane. Even though Chase knew two of his task force members were inside, there were no signs of life. He hit the garage remote and waited while the door opened. He pulled the truck into the empty garage and hit the remote again to close the door.

Grabbing his phone, he climbed from the vehicle and released Dash.

Dash hopped out and sniffed around but didn't alert.

Chase opened the door leading from the garage to the kitchen and said to Dash, "Quiet. Search."

Dash slipped inside without a sound and disappeared into the body of the house to do his job of searching for any sort of explosives.

Chase entered the house, awareness sliding over his skin.

"Hey, boss," Bennett's voice came at Chase through the darkness.

"Everything good here?" Chase asked, closing the garage door behind him, and letting his eyes adjust to the darkened interior.

Bennett sat at the kitchen counter, a darker shape against the inkiness of the unlit house. "We're good."

Off to the left, sitting at the table deep in the shadows of the dining room were Kyle and Ian.

"Any problems?" Kyle asked in a low tone.

"Maybe. I can't say I was followed but

you know that feeling when you're sure someone is…?"

"Oh, yes," Ian said. "Know it well."

"I received another text from the RMK," he told them. "Another threat against Trevor. He knows Trevor left the reunion not feeling well."

"We'll be ready when he comes," Bennett said in a hard tone.

Dash returned and sat at Chase's feet. Though it was a good sign the house wasn't rigged with explosives, the grip of dread didn't let up. Chase motioned for Dash to lay down near the back door. Since Trevor didn't have a dog, he couldn't let Dash be seen.

"I'm going to step out front and grab the newspaper I saw lying on the porch," Chase said. "If I was followed, I want the person to see Trevor and think he's unaware."

Bennett slipped off the stool and moved to stand next to Chase. "We have your back."

Without turning on the porch light, Chase

stepped out of the house. The eerie sensation of being watched triggered another quiver of alarm. But he didn't pause to scan the area. Better to let whoever was out there think he was oblivious. He bent to retrieve the copy of the *Elk Valley Daily Gazette* and then stepped back inside the dark house, shutting the door behind him with a soft snick. He reached for the wall switch and turned on the living room overhead light.

"There are NVGs on the recliner," Kyle told him, referring to night vision goggles, which would come in handy if the power went out.

Chase moved deeper into the room and switched on a table lamp next to the recliner facing the television. The curtains were all drawn. He pushed aside one of the living room curtains and then, keeping the Stetson and jacket on to make himself more of a target, Chase turned off the overhead light and sat in the recliner with his back to the window.

He tucked the NVGs against his side

and grabbed the remote for the TV. Whoever was out there would hopefully think Trevor was relaxing and watching television, completely oblivious to the threat against him.

The local news shifted to an older sitcom that didn't hold any appeal.

Chase removed his phone from his pocket and sent a text to Zoe, asking if everything was okay.

Within seconds, the ding of an incoming text showed her picture popping up.

He read her message with relief.

All good here. About to put Kylie down for the night. How's it going there?

He was about to answer when his phone rang. The sound was startling in the quiet of the house. The caller ID said it was Isla.

He hit the answer button and put the phone to his ear. "What can I do for you?"

"I just wanted to let you know that, through some clever maneuvering, if I say so myself, I managed to discover the person who hacked Garrett Watson's computer."

Chase sat straight up. His heart bumped with anticipation. "Who?"

"Haley Newton."

Haley Newton? Chase didn't quite know what to do with that information. Why would Haley hack Garrett's computer and send vicious posts to the reunion website? What was in it for her? Did she dislike the thought of the reunion so badly but was too afraid to own her opinion that she had to use Garrett to express her opposition? Why go to all that trouble?

"Chase, someone's outside," Ian's voice drew Chase's attention.

Finally.

"Good work," he said softly to Isla and hung up.

He would deal with Haley Newton later. Right now, he had the Rocky Mountain Killer to contend with.

Zoe held the phone, staring at the screen in anticipation of Chase's response. Her fingers tightened around the device when no answering text came through. Was he in trouble? Just not willing to answer the question? Had she overstepped? Worry chomped a hot trail through her, making the muscles of shoulders bunch with dread.

She tossed the phone onto the dresser and picked up Kylie from where she was playing on a learning mat laid out on the floor of the spare bedroom.

"Time for bed, sweetie pie," she cooed. She carried Kylie to the changing table. "How about bunnies tonight?" She picked up a fuzzy one-piece pajama set and shook it in front of Kylie.

Feeling a nudge at her thigh, Zoe glanced down to find Meadow's dog, Grace, had followed them into the guestroom and taken a seat next to her. She held up the jammies to the sleek-looking vizsla. "What do you think? Cute, right?"

Grace's tongue lulled out the side of her mouth and her thin tail thumped against the floor.

Zoe chuckled. "I'm not sure you understand me, Grace, but I am thankful you're here along with Meadow and Officer Steve."

Just as she got Kylie changed out of her outfit and into the fuzzy bunny pajamas, a scraping noise on the outside wall of the house grabbed her attention. Grace stood and stared at the window. Her tail stood straight out from her body and her front right paw was up. Her whole body looked like she was pointing at the window.

Zoe's heart jumped into her throat. She took a calming breath and hugged Kylie to her chest.

Given all that had happened in the past few days, she wasn't taking any chances. "Come on, Grace," she coaxed. "Out."

Grace ran ahead of her and straight to Meadow's side.

Zoe carried Kylie into the living room where Liam and Meadow were playing a card game. The lights were low, the curtains closed. On television a classic movie played. Officer Steve wasn't in the room. The kitchen was dark as well.

Meadow glanced up and immediately put down her cards and stood. "What's wrong?"

Grimacing but not willing to let it go, Zoe said, "I heard a noise outside. I'm being paranoid, I'm sure."

"Probably Officer Steve doing his rounds," Meadow said. "But to be on the safe side, I'll check in with him. Liam, take Zoe and Kylie into the bedroom and lock the door behind you."

Taking the vizsla with her, Meadow stepped out the front door.

"Okay, let's get into the guestroom." Liam hustled Zoe and Kylie out of the living room, careful to keep them away from the windows. They filed down the hall and into the guestroom. Zoe sat on the bed with Kylie snug in her arms. Liam paced a short path from the door to the crib.

After several moments of silence, Zoe said, "Shouldn't they be back in the house by now?"

The concern on Liam's face ratcheted up

Zoe's anxiety. Though he didn't say anything, she could tell he was worried.

What if something happened to Officer Steve or Meadow or Grace?

Please, Lord, keep them safe.

Sudden barking from outside sent shudders of fear sliding across Zoe's skin. Something was wrong. She jumped from the bed and crossed the room to the dresser where she'd left her phone. "I'm going to text Chase."

The door to the room burst open. Zoe spun around .

Standing in the doorway with a gun in her hand was Haley Newton.

FOURTEEN

His heart rate jumping, Chase remained seated in the recliner with his back to the window of the rental house. Someone was outside. The RMK? "Where is the person?"

"Back of the house," Kyle answered. "Going to comms."

Chase sensed rather than saw Bennett, Ian and Kyle taking defensive positions while staying in the shadows.

Slipping the earbud communication device out of the pocket of his flak vest and jamming it into his ear, he said in a whisper, "Test."

"Yes," Ian's voice sounded in Chase's ear along with a click.

"Yep," came Kyle's soft reply followed by another click.

"Good to go," Bennett said and added a click.

The clicks would be used when voices could reveal their positions.

His phone vibrated in his shirt pocket. No time to check it. The RMK was on the premises. At least, Chase hoped it was the serial killer.

Rising slowly from the chair, Chase turned off the TV and the table lamp, throwing the house into darkness.

"Dash," he called softly.

His partner moved silently to his side. For a big dog, Dash could do stealth well.

Putting on the night vision goggles, Chase moved down the hall toward the back bedroom with Dash at his heels. He froze as he heard a faint noise. Dash turned to face the closed door to their right. The would-be intruder had gained entry through the window of the second bedroom.

Patting his side quietly, Chase indicated for Dash to move with him past the room. They entered the master suite where

Chase took off the night vision goggles and turned the light on, shutting the door to the room. Dash stared at him, waiting for instructions.

Chase wanted the intruder to think Trevor was heading to bed.

Humming loud enough to be heard outside of the closed bedroom, Chase moved around the room as if oblivious to the fact that somebody had just entered the house uninvited.

In the attached bathroom, Chase turned on the shower. He moved back into the bedroom, closing the bathroom door behind him. He turned out the bedroom light, slipped on the NVGs, and waited. Dash's body quivered with energy next to him.

The click of the door handle being turned had Chase's senses jumping into alert mode.

The bedroom door swung open. A masked man stepped through the doorway. He was tall and broad-shouldered. There was something familiar about the set of his shoulders.

And there was no mistaking the weapon in the man's hand.

Chase allowed him to step all the way into the room and head toward the bathroom where supposedly Trevor was now vulnerable in the shower.

Three quick separate clicks in the earpiece alerted Chase that Bennett, Ian and Kyle were coming through the bedroom door behind the suspect.

Removing his NVG, Chase said, "Lights."

The moment the word left his mouth, he launched himself at the Rocky Mountain Killer.

The overhead flicked on.

Chase wrapped his arms around the man's waist and drove his shoulder into his kidneys. They both tumbled to the ground. Dash clamped his powerful jaw around the intruder's ankle, eliciting a scream of pain.

The gun went off. The sound echoed in the room. The bullet embedded in the wall.

Then the other men piled on. Ian wrestled the gun away from the intruder's hand.

Bennett whipped out zip ties and secured the man's arms behind his back.

"Out," Chase gave the signal for Dash to release his hold on the intruder. Dash complied and backed up but stood ready to attack again if need be.

Kyle quickly zip-tied the man's ankles together.

They flipped the intruder onto his back. He wore a black balaclava mask with only his blue eyes visible. Blond hair peeked out from the edges.

Fully expecting it to be Ryan York, Chase gripped the edge of the mask and ripped it off the man's face to reveal blue eyes wild with rage, a patrician nose and square jaw.

Evan Carr.

"Evan!"

Bennett's shocked tone drew Evan's gaze to his brother-in-law.

"You! Why are you here?" Evan sputtered.

Grabbing Evan's sleeve, Bennett pushed up the material to reveal the knife tattoo on Evan's right forearm. Bennett sat back on his heels. "Naomi is going to be devastated."

Chase didn't envy Bennett having to tell his wife, Naomi, that her brother was the Rocky Mountain Killer. That Evan, in his sick and twisted way, was avenging what had happened to his sister at the Young Rancher's Club dance ten years ago.

"I did it for her! They deserved to die," Evan screamed and bucked against the restraints. "Get Trevor out here. I want to look him in the eye and tell him he deserves to die."

"Trevor's not here," Chase said. "Ian, can you alert Sully? He's close by waiting for our call."

Ian nodded and walked out of the room, dialing his phone. He would bring the deputy marshal to the rental house to take Evan into custody.

"Where is Cowgirl?" Kyle asked.

"I want a deal," Evan demanded.

Of course, he did. Didn't all suspects say that when caught? "I'll talk to the state's attorney, but tell us where Cowgirl is now," Chase countered.

Evan clamped his lips together.

"Come on, Evan," Chase coaxed. "You set the puppies free. Don't leave Cowgirl to fend for herself. I know you love animals."

"They're better than people," Evan sneered.

Thinking of Garrett Watson, Chase was tempted to agree. "Where's Cowgirl?" Chase repeated. "Who's going to feed her? Take care of her?"

After a moment, Evan grumbled, "She's in the caves on the south side of Laramie Mountain."

"Got it," Kyle said, already heading out the door.

Chase remembered what Haley had said about an incident in the caves, so he pressed Evan, "What happened in the caves? Why did you kill Seth Jenkins, Brad Kingsley and Aaron Anderson ten years ago?" He knew, but he wanted to hear it from the killer.

Evan's face shuttered for a moment, becoming a mask. Was he going to deny it? But then, his gaze flared with pure venom. "Those rotten pigs humiliated my sister," Evan said. "Where's Trevor? He was one of them."

"Why kill Peter Windham? He was Naomi's friend," Bennett asked.

Evan turned his wild-eyed gaze to Bennett. "He knew what they were doing. He didn't warn her."

"You are so wrong," Bennett said. "Trevor did like Naomi, and Peter knew that he did."

"No, that's not true!" Spittle flew from Evan's mouth. Now that the man was talking, it was clear he wasn't going to stop. "Peter should have told Naomi and not let those pigs make fun of her."

"Okay, sure," Bennett conceded through clenched teeth. "He should have warned her but that didn't mean he deserved what you did to him."

"What about Henry Mulder and Luke Randall?" Chase asked of the two victims killed just months ago.

Evan practically growled as he struggled against them. "Pigs. They liked their pranks. I should have known they weren't my friends. They lured me to the cave and left me stranded, lost and alone all night. With rats!" A shudder of revulsion wracked Evan's body. "I was a kid!"

So, his history with these boys went back further than they'd previously thought. The group hadn't only mistreated Naomi but Evan himself.

Sully, along with two other deputies Chase didn't recognize, entered the room. "So, this is the infamous Rocky Mountain Killer?"

"He's confessed," Chase said and gestured to the Glock 19 lying on the floor. "I'm confident the bullets from that gun will match the ones taken from the victims."

"I like when it all comes together," Sully said. "Less headache that way."

The two deputies pulled Evan to his feet.

"Wait!" Chase remembered the devastation to Zoe's house and the town hall. The way Zoe had seemed so close to death in the hospital. He had to find out if they were connected. "Evan, why go after Zoe Jenkins?"

Evan wrinkled his nose. "Seth's sister?"

"Yes." A knot formed in Chase's gut. He wanted to reach out and wrap his hands around Evan's throat. "Why have you been trying to kill her? Why blow up her house? And the town hall? Where did you get the fentanyl?"

Evan shook his head. "I don't know what you're talking about. I don't mess with explosives. Too dangerous. Or drugs. And I wouldn't hurt a woman. Even if she is that pig's little sister."

The dread that had been dogging Chase intensified. If Evan wasn't the one targeting Zoe…then who? Haley Newton came to the forefront of his mind. She'd messed with the reunion's social media pages. But why? By her own admission, she was the one to break off the affair with Garrett when she realized he was married. Had she just been so against the reunion she thought to tank it with her nasty posts but hadn't wanted anyone to think it was her? Was she the one targeting Zoe? He couldn't come up with a motive.

"If you have more questions for the suspect, you'll have to ask them at the justice center in Laramie," Sully said.

Chase's phone vibrated in his pocket, reminding him he had incoming texts. Maybe Isla had found more information on why Haley Newton would hijack Garrett Watson's computer.

First, he thumbed open the text from Zoe.

911 hurry help

The words leapt out at Chase like a slap across the face.

"Something's happening at my house." He ran through the rental with Dash hot on his heels. In the garage, he hit the remote to open the door and he and Dash jumped into the cab of Trevor's truck.

Bennett climbed into the passenger seat. "Let's go."

Gratitude tightened a band around Chase's chest. He'd picked wisely when he'd brought his team together. He put the truck into reverse, backed out of the garage and maneuvered around the marshal's vehicles, then took off down the highway toward town.

Horrible scenarios marched through his mind. What was happening to Zoe? To Kylie? They had to be so scared. Guilt clogged his throat. If he'd looked at her text when it first came in, he could be there already making sure they were safe. But he'd put capturing the RMK ahead of the woman he loved. Taking down Evan Carr hadn't been as satisfying as Chase had imagined.

He pressed harder on the gas pedal. The truck strained beneath his grip. He had so much to make up for. He had to get to Zoe. His family. He had to tell Zoe he loved her.

Please, Lord, let me get there in time.

* * *

"Zoe?" Meadow called from the front of the house.

Haley put her finger to her lips and waved the gun at Zoe and Liam. She whispered, "Not a sound."

Zoe shifted, turning slightly so that she could lay Kylie in the crib, and dropped her phone onto the mattress. She quickly tucked the blanket around it. Chase would come once he saw her text. She clung to that knowledge with all the hope she could muster. She lifted a silent prayer, asking God to please make Chase hurry.

"I said don't move," Haley's hissing voice was sharp and tinged with something that made a shiver of fear race through Zoe.

The woman was not in her right mind.

For the life of her, Zoe couldn't begin to guess why Haley was trying to kill her. They'd been friendly before Zoe learned of Haley and Garrett's affair. Haley had apologized. She'd seemed truly contrite. This didn't make sense.

Zoe lifted her hands and turned so that

her body blocked Kylie from view. The baby snuggled into her blanket and cooed softly. The sound seared Zoe's heart.

Haley shut the door to the guest bedroom and locked it. A moment later, Meadow was banging on the door, and they could hear Grace barking.

"Zoe, it's Meadow. Are you okay? Where's Liam?"

Haley walked farther into the room, setting the duffel bag she carried at the foot of the crib. In a low whisper, she said to Zoe, "Tell her you're fine or I'll shoot her through the door."

"We're fine," Zoe called out, her voice shaky. "Liam's with me. We're putting Kylie down to bed. We'll be out shortly."

"Why is the door locked?" Meadow rattled the handle. "I can't find Officer Steve. I'm calling for backup."

Haley whipped around, aiming the gun at the door. She fired off two rounds. The wood of the door shattered around the bullets, but no sound came from the other side.

Zoe yelped. Liam rushed toward Haley,

but she swung the weapon and aimed at his chest, forcing him to a halt. He held up his hands and backed up.

"Oh no, you don't, pops," Haley said. "Zoe, open the duffel bag. There are zip ties in there. You secure old pops here."

Fearing that Meadow and her dog were hurt or worse, Zoe slowly bent down and unzipped the duffel bag. And found a silver galvanized pipe with lots of wires sticking out of it. A pipe bomb. Not that she'd ever seen one in real life but she couldn't turn on the news lately without some reference to these horrid devices. She fell back on her behind. "There's a bomb here."

"Get the zip ties and put them on. Hands and feet," Haley insisted. She alternated aiming the gun at Zoe, Kylie and Liam. "You'll do as I've said or one of you three is going to die with a bullet in the head."

Swallowing back the panic and fear, Zoe reached into the bag, careful not to jostle the scary-looking canister with wires protruding from it, and pulled out a handful of zip ties.

She moved to Liam, looping one around his wrists. Tears clouded her vision. She pulled the ties tight but not too tight for fear of hurting him. She did the same for his feet.

"It's okay," Liam murmured. "We'll get through this."

As much as she wanted to believe him, doubt crowded her mind.

Please, Lord, please, Lord, the prayer played on a loop in her brain.

"Now zip tie your own hands and feet together," Haley demanded.

Zoe frowned and threaded the ends of a zip tie together, then put her wrists through the zip tie.

"Use your teeth to tighten it," Haley said.

Bitter anger prompted Zoe to say, "You're the one who blew up my house. And the town hall."

"It's amazing the information on how to build a rudimentary bomb can be found on the internet. They get the job done though." With the gun, Haley emphasized her words, "Do it now."

Zoe used her teeth to tighten the zip tie, but she left it loose enough so that it wouldn't bite into her skin and would hopefully give her room to slip out if there was an opportunity to escape.

"You'll never get away with this," Liam said. "My son will stop you."

Haley swung the gun toward him. "Shut up!" She rushed forward and grabbed a roll of duct tape from the duffel. She tore off a piece and slapped it over Liam's mouth.

Risking that she'd silence her as well, Zoe pressed, "But the fentanyl? How? Why?"

Dropping the duct tape on the floor, Haley laughed. "Easy peasy. I bought it off the street. You'd be surprised what's available out there. When I saw you going into the ice cream parlor, I knew that was my chance. I offered to help old man Kimmer. He had his hands full. It was quite brilliant of me. I sprinkled the liquid drug on your sundae. By the time I set it in front of you it had seeped in. You never even tasted it."

Of course. Haley brought over the sundaes, arranging them on the table and Zoe had eaten it, none the wiser. "You stole Dr. Webb's car? And Garrett's truck? Again why?"

"It's easy to duplicate a key with the right tools." She scoffed. "I'm not dumb enough to use my own vehicle. Too bad your boyfriend has such quick reflexes. I would have taken you both out with the doc's car." She waved the gun again at Zoe. "Take a seat, both of you," Haley said.

Liam and Zoe sat on the edge of the bed. Zoe didn't point out she'd neglected to zip-tie her feet together.

Haley grabbed the duffel bag and pulled out a cell phone. The kind one buys at convenience stores.

"You should say your prayers," Haley said with a sneer.

Anxiety quaked through Zoe. "Haley, please don't do this," she pleaded. "At least, tell me *why* you're trying to kill me?"

The incredulous look on Haley's face would have been comical if the situation wasn't so terrifying. "Why do you think?"

The only reason that made any sense had Zoe's stomach clenching. "I assume this has something to do with Garrett." Her heart tore in two. "Did he pay you to do this?"

"Pay me? Of course not. He can't pay me anything. He can't marry me because of you," Haley practically screamed.

What? Confusion and anger raised Zoe's blood pressure even more. "Of course, he can marry you. We're legally divorced."

"You're bleeding him dry. You and the brat." Haley gestured with the gun toward the crib where Kylie had fallen asleep. "He's barely staying above water with all the money he shells out each month."

Zoe's breath stuttered. She hated seeing that weapon pointed at her daughter. Hated more to think this was all so cliché. "This is about the alimony and child support money?"

"He can't marry me while you're taking all his hard-earned income. That's what he said. I know if I get rid of you then he

can marry me." She sounded like a petu-
lant teenager.

Zoe's mouth dropped open, but she
couldn't form words. All of this destruction so she could be with Garrett.

Finding her voice, Zoe said, "Haley, I
will tell the judge I don't need the money
from Garrett anymore. Please, don't do
this. We can figure this out. You can have
Garrett with my blessing."

"Too late now. You should've refused the
money to begin with. You let that good
man go. Now he's going to be mine."

Refraining from rolling her eyes, Zoe
pointed out, "He cheated on me. And not
just with you."

"Maybe. But that was before he met me.
Not after," Haley insisted. "We love each
other. Now we can be together." Her eyes
glazed over as if a memory surfaced. Her
voice softened. "I was robbed of a future
with my first love, Brad."

Zoe didn't want to feel empathy for this
woman over the fact Brad had been murdered by the RMK.

Clarity returned to Haley's gaze. "But I will get to be with Garrett." Haley reached into the duffel and lifted the bomb carefully out of the bag. To Zoe's horror, Haley set it inside the crib with Kylie. "If you try to lift Kylie out of this crib, the bomb will go off."

Liam yelled a protest behind the duct tape covering his mouth.

"No!" Zoe jumped to her feet. "What if she moves?"

Haley shrugged, a malicious smile crossing her face. "Hopefully, she's not a restless sleeper. Either way the bomb is going off." She reached into her pocket and pulled out a phone. "I can remotely detonate the bomb, as well." She waved the gun again at Zoe. "Sit down. No more talking."

She moved to the door. "I'm coming out of the room now. Deputy Ames, if you're still out there, know that I will kill all of us with one press of a button."

There was no answer from outside the bedroom door. Zoe's heart plummeted.

Grace didn't even bark. Tears streamed down Zoe's face.

Cautiously, Haley opened the door. She peeked out, then flung the door wide. The hallway was empty. Zoe breathed a sigh of relief. Hopefully, Meadow had gone for backup. But they had to get to Haley before she pressed that button on her phone.

Haley backed out of the room then turned and ran.

Chase's phone buzzed again. The engine of the truck whined with the way he was pushing the vehicle to go faster.

A glance at his phone revealed it was Meadow calling. He tossed the cell to Bennett who hit the answer button and put it on speaker so they both could hear.

The tires of the truck hugged the pavement as he drove. They'd passed the destroyed town hall. "Tell me!"

"There's an intruder in the house," Meadow said. "I took gunfire. I can't find Officer Steve. Zoe, your dad and the baby are locked in the spare bedroom. The gunfire came from that room. I'm outside waiting for backup."

Fear pelted Chase like giant balls of hail. "Five minutes out." Terror at losing the people he loved most in the world a second time stole his breath. He struggled to suck in oxygen and fought the dizziness of grief and pain.

"I put an alert out to the team at the Elk Valley PD. Whoever's inside the room won't get away," Meadow said.

But they could kill his family. He blinked rapidly to keep his focus on the road.

"Let Ian know," Bennett said. "He's still at the rental house."

Remembering Isla's phone call, Chase said, "Do you think it's Haley Newton?"

"I don't know," Meadow replied. "I didn't see the person. They slipped inside while I was checking on Officer Steve. Zoe heard a noise outside."

The thought crossed Chase's mind that maybe Officer Steve was in on it, but he had been with them when the person had

tried to run Zoe down in Dr. Webb's stolen car.

The sound of gunfire erupted on Meadow's end of the call.

"Meadow!" Chase and Bennett both
yelled.

Breathing heavy, she said, "Taking more
gunfire. It's coming from the front window."

"Don't fire back, you might hit Zoe,
Kylie or my dad." Chase took a curve too
fast. The truck slid but he managed to right
the vehicle and proceed.

"Rocco and Ashley are here now,"
Meadow said.

"Stay back!" a female voice screamed.
She said more but Chase couldn't make
out the words.

"Meadow, what's happening?" Chase demanded to know.

"A woman is at the front window,"
Meadow said. "She's demanding we stay
back or she's going to blow up the house."

FIFTEEN

The echoing sounds of gunfire rang in Zoe's head. With each shot, she flinched. Her gaze jumped to Kylie. The baby still slept. Zoe sent up a grateful prayer that her daughter was apparently impervious to the noise.

Liam made a sound behind the duct tape. Maneuvering herself so she could reach his mouth with her bound hands, Zoe carefully peeled the tape off his face.

"I appreciate that you didn't tighten these zip ties super tight, but I can't get out of them," Liam groused as he struggled to pull his wrists from the restraints. His skin was turning red and raw from his efforts.

Zoe jumped up from where she sat on the bed and took a quick peek out the doorway where Haley had disappeared down the hall. She could see Haley at the front window, gun in one hand and the phone in the other. She'd slid the window open and fired at someone outside.

Where was Meadow? Was that who Haley was shooting at?

Zoe had to get Liam and Kylie out of the house. Fast. And in one piece. Though how, she didn't know. What had Chase said? One problem at a time.

First, she needed to barricade the door to prevent Haley from returning and then they had to ditch the restraints. Zoe moved cautiously to the door and shut it, praying Haley wouldn't hear the click. "Can you hop quietly over to the dresser?" she asked Liam.

With his feet bound, he moved slowly to the dresser. Together, they pushed the large piece of furniture in front of the door. Liam wobbled, nearly losing his balance. Zoe gripped his arm, holding him steady, and helped him back to the edge of the bed.

Zoe grabbed the diaper bag where she'd stashed a nail filing kit. Though she couldn't separate her hands, she could still use them enough to open the bag. She rooted around inside until she found the zipped case. She breathed a sigh of gratefulness to see the small set of manicure scissors inside. She pulled them from the case and hurried to Liam.

"These will have to do," she said.

She worked on the restraints holding his wrists together. Bit by bit the little blades of the scissors chopped through the plastic until finally it gave way. Liam grabbed the scissors from her hands and went to work on the tie around her own wrists. She kept the tension taut on the plastic until it finally broke apart.

Liam then went to work on the restraints around his ankles. Zoe ran to the crib. But she was afraid to pick up Kylie.

Had Haley been telling the truth that if Kylie moved the bomb would go off?

Kylie twitched in her sleep, sending Zoe's heart pounding so hard she thought she might crack a rib. She put a hand on her baby's back, just barely touching her so as not to add more weight to the mattress. Kylie stilled beneath her touch.

There had to be something they could do. Liam joined her at the end of the crib.

"I can try to disarm this," Liam said.

"Are you trained?" Zoe asked with hope.

Liam made a face. "No. Chase is, though."

Zoe's phone was laying inside the crib underneath Kylie's blanket. Did she dare reach in and remove it? Would doing so blow them all to bits?

"I can't get my phone without risking our lives."

A face appeared at the bedroom window that looked out over the backyard. Zoe swallowed a scream the second recognition took hold.

Chase.

Zoe's knees nearly buckled but she managed to stay upright without grabbing the edge of the crib.

Liam hustled around the crib to slide open the window. He and Chase worked to pop the screen out. Then Dash jumped through the window and landed on the floor.

"Silence," Chase commanded the dog.

Dash folded himself into a laying position, but his attention stayed riveted on the bomb in the crib. He didn't make a sound. Even his tail remained still and upright. But Zoe could feel the tension in the dog. It matched her own.

Liam quickly explained the situation with the bomb and Haley. "The woman is clearly unstable."

"I'll worry about her after I get you three to safety. Dad, help Zoe out," Chase said reaching his arms up for her.

Zoe shook her head. No way was she leaving Kylie with a bomb in her crib. "I can't leave without my daughter. I won't."

Liam grasped her biceps. "You have to trust Chase. I know this is hard. But he is our only hope of getting Kylie out of this alive."

Zoe's gaze bounced from Liam to Chase to Kylie. She would do anything for her daughter. Even relinquish her baby's well-being to the man she'd come to love. Her breath caught but there was no time to process the ramifications of loving Chase.

She pushed against Liam, saying, "You first."

She would never forgive herself if Chase's father perished.

Liam shook his head. "You know I won't go until you do."

She could tell from the stubborn jut of his chin, so like his son's, that he would not budge unless she agreed. She nodded. Liam released his hold on her and hustled her to the window.

With a longing glance at her child, Zoe sent up a desperate plea to God above to protect them all. *Please protect Kylie.*

She climbed over the window ledge and practically fell into Chase's waiting arms. She clung to him for moment. Then relinquished her hold so he could help his father out. The backyard was dark behind them, the light from the room illuminating a small stretch of grass under their feet.

Gripping Chase's hand, Zoe said, "Please, save my baby."

He squeezed her hand and without another word heaved himself up and over the window ledge into the room.

Zoe went on tiptoe, grasping the edge of the window so that she could see over the ledge.

With her heart in her throat, she watched as Chase approached the crib.

Careful not to jostle the crib, Chase studied the bomb laying on the mattress just a mere two inches away from Kylie's little body. The baby slept soundly. Chase sent up a grateful praise to God for the huge favor.

It looked like the bomb had a small bubble level attached to wires on either side of the level's frame.

Taking a deep breath, he reminded himself he'd trained for situations like this. But he'd never had to operate under such dire circumstances. His inclination would be to wait for the bomb squad. The techs who handled this on a daily basis would have no trouble. But there was no time to wait for them to arrive from Laramie.

Meadow and the others were keeping Haley distracted, but she might return to the guest bedroom at any moment and discover it barricaded. Chase had no doubt she would press the send button on the cell phone she carried.

Even if he managed to detach the scale from the bomb, there was still the chance she could detonate before he could remove Kylie. He rushed back to the window. "How much does Kylie weigh?"

"At her last pediatrician appointment, she weighed eighteen pounds, four ounces," Zoe said. "Why? What are you thinking?"

It was crazy and risky what he was thinking. Something only done in movies. But if he could find something that weighed roughly the same as Kylie—no, he would need another set of hands. And there was no way he was bringing Zoe or his dad back into the room.

His best option was to disconnect the

scale from the bomb, get Kylie out then take down Haley.

Shaking out his hands to rid himself of the tremors created by the fear sliding along his flesh, he squatted down to get a better look at the bomb. He traced the lines of wire to the cylindrical pipe they were attached to. Underneath the bomb was the receiving cell phone that would detonate the explosive if triggered. This bomb looked similar to the one that had taken out the town hall building.

He drew back in surprise. The two wires coming out of the scale seemed to be the same wire. A trick? A way to get Zoe and his father to cooperate?

What she that devious? Or rather, that clever.

Carefully, with his fingers hovering over the wires, Chase traced them all the way around the device till his fingertips touched. Yes, it was the same wire attached to both ends of the level.

"Okay, Lord, I know I've been mad at you and taken my anger and frustration out on you, but somewhere deep inside I have at least a mustard seed of faith that tells me you will protect Kylie. I don't know why you didn't protect Elsie and Tommy," his voice hitched as he was slammed with emotion.

"I don't believe there's a reason for everything." That platitude people had given him after the death of his wife and child made him so angry. "But I do believe bad things happen to good people. That's what happened to Elsie and Tommy. They were good and a bad thing happened to them. Please don't let a bad thing happen here."

Chase grasped either end of the wire. "Amen. Please Lord."

Holding his breath, he yanked both wires out of the level.

Nothing happened.

He bowed his head in relief, but only for a second.

They weren't out of the woods. Quickly, he gathered Kylie to his chest. Disturbed, she let out a cry. He stuck his pinky into her mouth, and she began to suck.

Swiftly, he lunged for the window and handed Kylie out to Zoe's waiting arms.

"Get as far away as you can," he said.

"What about you and Dash?" Zoe said, her gaze piercing him.

"I have to take down Haley," he said.

"Please, be careful," Zoe pleaded.

"I will." Chase straightened away from the window and started to turn.

"Wait, Chase!" Zoe whispered.

He quickly stuck his head back to the window, afraid something else was wrong. "Zoe?"

"I love you," she said.

Stunned, he could only stare.

His father urged her away from the house. She turned and ran toward safety with Kylie held close. They ran through the backyard to the back gate. The same gate Chase had come through moments before.

Shaking his head to dislodge the bombshell Zoe had just dropped on him, he refocused on what he needed to do.

He scrubbed Dash behind the ears, and said, "Time to work."

Dash seemed confused for a moment. His gaze went to the bomb and then to him. Chase moved to the door of the spare room and pushed the dresser out of the way. When he stepped out of the room, he heard Dash jump off the bed. The dog brushed up against his side. Thankfully, the rest of the house was in shadows as he and Dash crept forward.

When they reached the opening to the living room, he spotted Haley standing in front of the open side of the sliding window taking pot shots at the officers outside through the screen. She paused and crouched to reload her weapon with bullets she pulled from her jacket pocket. She appeared none the wiser that he'd freed her hostages.

Chase squatted down, waiting for her to stand up again. When she did and resumed her position with her back to him, he whispered into Dash's ear, "Bite."

Dash didn't hesitate. The dog sprang forward, running silently down the hall, aimed at Haley's back. Chase followed steps behind his partner. Dash launched himself at Haley, his large front paws hitting her upper back and throwing her face forward against the glass of the sliding window. Chase lunged for the hand holding the phone. He bent her wrist back, forcing her to drop the device.

She screamed and twisted, trying to get the gun in her other hand aimed at Chase. He shoved her harder and sent her crashing through the open side of the window, taking the screen with her. Chase barely managed to keep from following her out.

She landed on the rosebushes, stunned and screaming with pain from the bare bushes' thorns tearing into her skin. The gun fell from her hand. Then the task force team members and all of Elk Valley PD descended on her.

Chase was confident they would take her into custody without incident. He doubted she would be able to move after that landing.

He and Dash went out the front door and handed off the phone to Ophelia.

"The bomb's in the crib in the guest bedroom. The only room with the light on." He told her.

Once again, she'd brought the TCV and, with help from Kyle, rolled the total containment vessel into the house.

"Chase!"

Zoe's yell drew his attention. Zoe, Kylie and his father hustled down the sidewalk. Along with them was Officer Steve.

He and Dash ran to meet them.

"We found him behind some bushes in the house down the street," Liam said. "He has a nasty contusion on the back of his head. He needs to see a paramedic."

Liam led a groggy Officer Steve away.

Chase swept Zoe and Kylie into his arms. "Haley's been taken into custody. You don't have to fear her anymore."

Zoe buried her face into his chest. "She wanted to marry Garrett but apparently, he said he couldn't afford to marry her because he had to pay me alimony and child support. I don't think Garrett was aware of what she was doing." She shuddered in his arms. "Thank you. Thank you again for saving our lives."

He pulled back so he could look into her beautiful and sweet face so full of heartache and hope. "I would do anything for the women I love. I love you, Zoe. And I love Kylie. I hope one day we can be a family."

He held his breath. What would she say?

Tears streamed down Zoe's face. She lifted up on tiptoe to press her lips against his. The world slowed and all he wanted was this moment to last forever.

Kylie squirmed between them, babbling, "Dododododo."

They laughed, breaking the kiss, but held onto each other.

Then Dash was there, squeezing his way between them as if he, too, wanted to get in on a hug.

"Is that a yes?" Chase whispered. "Will you marry me?"

"Yes! A thousand times yes," Zoe said.

"Sorry, I didn't mean to overhear, but I did and I'm so excited," Liam said wrapping them all in his arms. "This is going to be fun."

EPILOGUE

"Welcome, everyone," Zoe said from the front of the large event tent erected in the middle of Elk Valley Park. Twinkle lights strung from the overhead support poles provided a soft glow for the late afternoon Thanksgiving feast about to commence. Propane-fueled heaters had been brought in to keep the November chill at bay.

The long tables were decorated with brocade fabric runners in bright harvest colors. Battery-powered tea lights surrounded by fall foliage made of silk, and small gourds in various shades of orange, brown, yellow and red made for a festive autumn-themed gathering. Seated at several of the tables were the task force members and their families, plus their K-9 partners lying at the feet of their handlers.

Deputy US Marshal Sully Briggs and Chase's boss, Cara Haines, who had flown in from Washington, DC, for this evening of celebration, had taken their seats among the task force members, but notably at a distance from each other. Chase had noticed some tension between them but refrained from probing into their business. He knew they had some sort of history but did not know the details.

More tables were occupied by the Elk Valley Police Department and other honored guests, such as Mayor Singh and his family, and Pastor Jerome. This was a private event for those close to the investigation, but plans were in the works for a large town function in the spring to celebrate and heal from all that the RMK had put the community through.

But Chase only had eyes for the woman he would soon call his wife. His heart expanded, brimming with love for Zoe and

Kylie. Every passing day since they'd brought both the RMK and Haley Newton to justice, he'd counted himself the most blessed man alive. Actually, long before then, but he'd only admitted his love for Zoe to himself and to her on that late October night. His happiness had grown exponentially since.

"Okay, you all, settle down," Sadie said from her place next to Zoe.

Chase bounced Kylie on his knees, waiting for the two women to say their piece before it was his turn.

"We thank you all for coming to our inaugural Thanksgiving dinner," Zoe said.

"Tonight, we will offer both traditional Thanksgiving fare and several healthier options," Sadie said with a smile.

Cheers went up all around the space.

Zoe added, "But first, Chase has a few words to say." Zoe's smile was tender and filled with love.

For a moment, Chase was lost in that smile and the depth of love in her eyes.

Then his father was taking Kylie from

his arms. Beside Liam, Martha Baldwin bumped his shoulder. "It's my turn, you know."

Liam laughed and handed Kylie over to the older woman. They'd become quite the item, his dad and Martha.

Chase moved to stand next to Zoe. She squeezed his arm, her touch lingering for a moment, and it took all his willpower not to pull in for a kiss. Then she and Sadie took their seats.

"We have a lot to be thankful for," Chase began. He could hardly believe how his life had changed in the past nine months. Though he still missed Elsie and Tommy, the hollow space in his heart had healed and he had allowed love to fill him again with hope.

"The Mountain Country K-9 Unit accomplished what we set out to do." He couldn't keep the pride out of his voice. "We brought the Rocky Mountain Killer to justice. The US Marshals have him in protective custody, awaiting trial. We all know it could be a while before he faces his sentencing. But he is no longer anonymous. He is no longer the mystery bogeyman haunting this town."

The applause was deafening inside the enclosed space.

His chest swelled with pride. After nine long months, his team had put their killer behind bars. It was still hard to believe Evan Carr had been behind the terror the whole time. So much destruction in the name of revenge.

Chase's gaze met Naomi's across the tent. Holding her son in her lap, with Bennett's arm around her, she smiled. But there was a sadness in her eyes. It would be a long road for her, seeing the fallout of her brother's actions. But the MCK9 unit would be there for her.

When the applause died down, Chase continued, "We recovered Cowgirl safe and sound. Our expert dog trainer, Liana, has been working hard to retrain her." Chase nodded to the task force dog trainer. "Liana, would you like to say a few words?"

From her place at the table, Liana stood.

"Despite the demons that drove Evan Carr to commit his horrendous acts, he was kind to Cowgirl and her puppies. Our veterinarian has given them all a clean bill of health. Cowgirl's behind in training, but she's eager to please and ready to learn. She's going to make a great therapy dog. And the puppies are showing promise as well."

Another round of applause erupted. Another thing to be grateful for—all the dogs were safe and back in the task force's care. And they'd finally located Ryan York. The marshal's service had found him hiding out in the back waters of Florida. He'd said he was afraid that the Rocky Mountain Killer would come after him. He'd made a life for himself in Florida and would remain there.

Chase's gaze sought the team's technical analyst. "Isla, I believe you have something you'd like to share?"

Isla jumped up, excitement oozing off her. Her grandmother sat beside her beaming.

"Thanks to someone—" Isla sent Chase a

meaningful glance. "Who called child protective services and the adoption agency and convinced them to reopen my case, my dream of being a mother is about to come true."

More applause erupted.

Chase shook his head and waved away their complimentary praise. "I only did what was right. Plus, once we captured Lisa and it became clear she had been the one sabotaging Isla, there was no reason for CPS or the adoption agency to not approve of Isla." He paused and turned his attention back to Isla. "Go ahead. Tell them."

He would not take her thunder way.

Looking happier than he'd seen her in the whole time they'd worked together when he'd brought her on as the team's technical analyst, Isla said, "I've been cleared by CPS. And the adoption agency called to inform me that the little toddler, Enzo, who I had hoped to foster and adopt before Lisa's sabotage, had been placed with another family but things didn't work out and they asked if I was still available to foster

him with the intention of adopting him."
She bounced on her heels. "Of course, I
said yes! I should have him within the next
few weeks."

This time the celebration wasn't con-
tained to applause as several people
jumped up to hug Isla.

Chase waited, letting the merriment die
down naturally.

Once everyone had settled again, he said,
"I have one more huge announcement to
make before we can eat."

"My stomach is rumbling," Bennett
called out.

People laughed.

Chase held up his hand. "You're going
to want to hear this." He turned his attention to Cara. She nodded. He raised an
eyebrow, silently asking if she wanted to
make the announcement. She shook her
head and with a flick of her hand gestured
for him to proceed.

It gave him pleasure to say, "Because our
team was so successful, the FBI has asked
us to remain active."

A cheer went up.

"But what about those of us who live in other states?" Hannah yelled out. Trevor grinned next to her.

Once again, Chase held up his hand, waiting for silence. "Our headquarters will be based here in Elk Valley, but those of you who live elsewhere can remain where you are and be mobile."

Grateful smiles and nods met his announcement. And Chase took in each one of them. Ashley standing in the corner with Cade. Bennett still holding Naomi. Selena beaming at her fiancé, Finn. Kyle taking Ophelia's hand in his. Meadow and Ian exchanging jokes with Rocco. Trevor leaning over to kiss Hannah's cheek.

Chase turned his attention to Zoe and Sadie. "Ladies, I think it's time to roll out the Thanksgiving feast."

Zoe and Sadie disappeared through one of the tent flaps to the mobile truck waiting on the other side. Chase made his way to the table where he sat next to the empty seat Zoe would take. Liam and Martha joined him, putting Kylie in the high chair between Chase's and Zoe's seats.

The tent flaps parted and a team of volunteers from town proceeded to lay out the feast on an empty table in the center of the tent space.

Pastor Jerome stood to say a quick blessing, asking God's protection over the task force, all the people of Elk Valley and all the people of the country who the task force would one day help. "And God bless this food as we give thanks for Your blessings. Amen."

Chase met Zoe's gaze over Kylie's head, counting their love among their blessings.

* * * * *

If you enjoyed this story, don't miss
Christmas K-9 Guardians
the final book in the
Mountain Country K-9 Unit series!
And discover the first eight books,
available now:

Baby Protection Mission
by Laura Scott, April 2024

Her Duty Bound Defender
by Sharee Stover, May 2024

Chasing Justice
by Valerie Hansen, June 2024

Crime Scene Secrets
by Maggie K. Black, July 2024

Montana Abduction Rescue
by Jodie Bailey, August 2024

Trail of Threats
by Jessica R. Patch, September 2024

Tracing a Killer
by Sharon Dunn, October 2024

Search and Detect
by Terri Reed, November 2024

Christmas K-9 Guardians
by Lenora Worth and Katy Lee,
December 2024

Available only from
Love Inspired Suspense
Discover more at LoveInspired.com

Dear Reader,

I hope you have enjoyed the Mountain Country K-9 Unit continuity series. Giving FBI Special Agent Chase Rawlston a happily ever after was a pleasure. He had deep pain that needed to be addressed before he could reopen his heart to love. And the perfect person to make him want to take the chance was Zoe and her little girl, Kylie. Zoe had her own issues to work through to allow herself to take a second chance at love.

With someone targeting Zoe and the Rocky Mountain Killer still on the loose, Chase had his hands full trying to protect everyone and bring the criminals to justice. But in the end, he succeeded, and he and Zoe found love as they made a new family.

But we're not done with our task force. Look for the Christmas two-in-one, *Christmas K-9 Guardians*, featuring more of the men and women of the Mountain Country K-9 Unit available next month.

Until next time, may God guide you and give you strength every day.

Terri Reed